A TANGLE OF VINES

Patricia Bragdon

BookLocker
Trenton, Georgia

Print ISBN: 978-1-958877-77-7
Ebook ISBN: 979-8-88531-346-9

Published by BookLocker.com, Inc., Trenton, Georgia.

Printed on acid-free paper.

The characters and events in this book are fictitious. Any similarity to real persons, living or dead, is coincidental and not intended by the author.

BookLocker.com, Inc.
2022

First Edition

Library of Congress Cataloguing in Publication Data
Bragdon, Patricia
A Tangle of Vines by Patricia Bragdon
Library of Congress Control Number: 2022917823

For Bob and Caroline

*A diplomat is a man who thinks twice
before he says nothing.*
Edward Heath

Table of Contents

Chapter One

Jakarta, Indonesia, 1968

After ten thousand miles and three weeks of sea and air travel on the way from Washington to Jakarta, the Fairchilds were tired. "Almost there, Ruth! The end is in sight -- well, the end of the beginning anyway." Mark Fairchild spoke quietly to his wife Ruth, as the plane came to a stop and the crew began to open the doors. Heat rushed in, full of humidity and the scents of an old tropical city — dust, fetid canal water, sewage, vegetation, sweat-- in an overwhelming miasma.

There were only a few passengers on the plane, and the Fairchilds gathered their belongings slowly and descended the roll-up stairs to the tarmac, Zoe their cat quiet in her carrier. Immigration and Customs went fast, with no complications — bless those diplomatic passports, thought Ruth gratefully—and they were quickly out in a hot shabby waiting area, noisy and crowded.

"Hey, Fairchilds! Over here!" someone yelled over the din and they were engulfed in a little group of greeters — "Give me your baggage claim tickets" from a burly man, red-faced, balding, and sweating copiously in the suffocating building "I'm Joe Forrest. Welcome to Jakarta, this is Bunahwan, our driver, let's get outta here. Car's outside, you must be tired, let's get you home."

The black van was generously air-conditioned; Zoe's box went in first, and she settled down to sleep. The luggage was loaded — just a couple of large suitcases, most of their belongings would come later by sea—and the van pulled out into the chaos of daily life in Jakarta in 1968. Heavy traffic of cars, trucks and bicycle rickshaws, rough pavement, incessant honking, and crowds of people pushing into the road delayed their passage — reminders that the island of Java was one of the poorest and most heavily populated places in the world.

Mark and Ruth were quiet on the ride to their new quarters. Joe, still mopping his bald head, kept up a steady monologue, pointing out interesting sights "Over there, see the chairs under the flamboyant trees? Those belong to the outdoor barbers. They usually work in the early morning when it's cool — shave, haircut, and gossip. Barbers all the same everywhere, I guess." Old barber chairs set in casual rows, mirrors nailed to tree trunks, people sitting in the shade with kids buzzing around them, all made for a picturesque spot.

At last, the van pulled into the driveway of a house where a group of servants stood at the door smiling and waving. Weary, Ruth thought of films with the loyal servants waiting outside the castle door for the arrival of the master and his family, although this was an Asian version and the servants were strangers, still to be met and evaluated. How do I do this? I have never had a servant other than a weekly cleaner, never lived a life where others performed services for me and depended on me for their livelihood. I wish Leonie were here. My big sister--why did she have to go? She always knew what to do. If it weren't for Mark's yen to see the world, we'd still be in Oak Park and my sister might still be alive.

Although this was the Fairchild's third post, Ruth still wasn't sure about the gypsy caravan aspect of life in the foreign service. From the outside, it had seemed exciting and invigorating, new places, new people, new challenges. Hard to be bored and intolerant living this way, she had thought, but she had begun to see a different and less agreeable side lately. The structured social hierarchy of embassy life troubled her now, with a person's rank determining so many things—the size of the family's quarters, the people with whom you could socialize, the events to which you would be invited, and the unspoken but clear message that you and your family must obey your superior officer and even his wife. The competition and the gossip of such a small inbred community could be vicious and inescapable.

Feminist voices were beginning to be heard frequently though still faintly in foreign service posts around the globe, where younger wives were beginning to chafe at the restrictions placed on them. "Two for the price of one", the State Department's policy of requiring unpaid labor from wives, was being called into question often now, and the section on an officer's performance appraisal grading his wife was widely mocked and ridiculed, as was the "marriage rule" preventing a married woman from becoming a foreign service officer. You know, Leonie would have fought that rule, Ruth thought. She would have done everything she could to bring it down, to help women to achieve parity, and discomfort the fossils in State. I wish she were with me now. But, thanks to that bully of a director, she had been on the road in a snowstorm, on the way to a ballet performance. Yes, she had loved dance. Yes, she had loved being part of the company. But no-one should have had the power to force that group out into terrible weather just because they needed the ticket money. And she died there in the cold and darkness.

Absorbed in her thoughts, Ruth suddenly realized that Joe, still chatty, was opening the car door now, fussing around like an over-solicitous real estate agent, and pointing out features of the house: "It's new! It's nicer than the older houses here. You've got two bedrooms, a living room and a dining porch, plus a screened porch. Come in, come in, let me show you around!"

Her first impression was of enervating heat in the house. Wobbly fans hung from high ceilings, wide-open windows with bars — ornamental ones, but bars nonetheless. Walking to the window, Ruth could see a mango tree outside, with nothing else in the garden but grass surrounded by a white stucco fence, barred also. The civil disturbances were two years past; surely things were settled now, she hoped, and there was less need for bars. Inside were pale cream terrazzo floors, white plaster walls, and heavy dark wood doors with solid locks to close at night.

The two fans spun shakily on long stalks from the faraway ceiling, a large potted palm stood in a corner with a note attached — "Welcome from the Admin Office!", standard government-issue Danish modern furniture, we had that sideboard at our last post, she thought ..., two enormous bedrooms, air-conditioned to Arctic chill, two generic bathrooms, everything pleasant and anonymous, seeming to wait for Mark and her to bring it into focus with their personalities.

Joe, still overly-friendly, nattered on without pause for breath or thought, and she heard Mark's voice interrupting him "Are these all the keys? I count three outside doors-- shouldn't there be another key?"

"Yeah" replied Joe "seems to be one missing--should be three, only two here... not sure which door...I'll check on that later... Car will pick you up tomorrow morning, Mark ... Ruth, my wife will come by ... there's stuff in the refrigerator ... "People swirled around them and, at last, she sat down and said "Please — I don't feel well. I think it's the heat." and the crowd melted, leaving her, Mark, and the caged cat alone in the living room.

They sat quietly for a while, trying to feel the ambiance of the house; there was subdued chatter from the kitchen and a rear courtyard where the servants were now congregated, and the cat suddenly yowled; she needed to get OUT of the box. Mark got up and let her out into the living room from her traveling cage, then returned to the sofa next to Ruth. He took her hand and said "So? Here at last. Thoughts?"

"Oh, relieved to be here. Wondering how we'll fit in, what it'll be like."

Mark sighed, and responded "Yeah, I know. A bit strange, walking into someone else's job this way, especially after that interview at the Department when they told me why we were pulled out of Paris so suddenly, and the hints of funny business going on here." Ruth thought -- well, at least it got us away from the "funny business" going on

13

with you and chère Marie Ange in Paris! Innocent, I'm sure, but given a bit more time ...

Mark, a US foreign service officer, had been assigned to Jakarta to replace the former economic counselor who had disappeared in a swimming accident some months earlier. A group of friends — mostly staff members from the US embassy and the UN mission in Jakarta—had been spending a weekend at a beach resort on the Indian Ocean. After a boozy, convivial dinner, some members of the group decided to go for a swim in the ocean despite the dangerous reputation of the beach. It was a moonlit night, and the breaking waves were full of luminescence, every splash producing magical sparkles. The group swam for a while enjoying the magic, but soon realized that the tide was rising and the pull of the current was dangerously strong. When the group re-assembled on the beach, one of their number was missing — Paul Faber, the embassy economic counselor. No-one could remember seeing him after they entered the water. Accounts were confused, some people had had too much to drink, and it wasn't clear how many people had actually been in the water. Investigations were inconclusive, and Paul's body had never been found. Inevitably there was gossip.

They sat quietly for a while, then "Joe seems alright," Mark said reflectively, "but I don't know--what was all that business with the key? Could be something not so pleasant under all that hail-fellow hotshot realtor stuff. Well, let's see what the welcome committee put in the refrigerator, and if there's a drink. At least it won't be airline food!"

"Was Joe one of the swimming party that night?" Ruth asked.

"I don't know", Mark replied as he headed for the kitchen. "Seems to be a whole lot of confusion about that. Hey, there's beer in here! Want one?"

Chapter Two

Visitors

The working day begins early in the tropics. The embassy van gathered Mark into its load of bureaucrats at 6.30 the next morning, while the cook waited at the kitchen door for orders from Ruth — what does the family want to eat for the day? And for Zoe the cat? Suleiman, the cook, was stropping a large knife on a leather strap as he waited for a list. Ruth hastily checked the refrigerator for any supplies already put in by the welcome committee and wrote a list for Suleiman, who took it and disappeared hurriedly out the door. He left his knife on the counter; Ruth, noticing it, wondered why he felt he needed to be sharpening it so theatrically, and why he hadn't taken it with him. Zoe, stretching and chirping, strolled into the kitchen; she had passed the night in the air-conditioned bedroom with Ruth and Mark, and was ready to get acquainted with her new post.

The morning went fast for Ruth, learning the names of the soft-voiced servants who would work for them, and exploring the house. In addition to "their" rooms, there was a large rear courtyard with several small servants' rooms and an Indonesian bathroom along the rear wall, and a tall damp-stained concrete wall at the side. The house was roofed in red tiles, curved to fit over one another and, as Ruth would discover, fragile and prone to breaking.

Five servants had been employed for them by the embassy's administrative office in advance of their arrival — two men and three women. The men servants wore simple white cotton trousers and shirts, while the women wore the graceful female Indonesian garb of *kain* —long batik-printed sarong-like skirts, with cotton or lace blouses called *kebaya*.

Ruth heard a car in the driveway, and a servant ran to open the door for a guest. In swept a tall blonde carrying an extravagant bunch of orchids which she thrust at Ruth, saying "Welcome to the armpit of Asia! I'm Gwendolyn Edwards but everyone calls me Gwen, my husband is a political officer at the embassy, and we live just down the street. Don't be too impressed by the orchids — they are common as marigolds here! May I have a glass of water, please? And then, I will answer all your questions and probably some you haven't thought of yet."

Ruth, a bit overwhelmed by the visitor's personality and appearance — cat's-eye glasses, backcombed dyed blonde hair, clanking gold bangles, and a vividly patterned mini dress — started for the kitchen to fetch the water but Siti, the youngest of the servants, was there with it and another servant had taken the orchids, so she and Gwen settled themselves on nearby chairs and Gwen rattled on with the usual making-acquaintance questions:

"Where are you coming from?" She got right down to business.

"Mark was posted to Paris, to the OECD. He's an economist, so it was a great place for him. I loved it, who wouldn't?"

"Did you mind leaving? I mean — Paris!"

"Yes and no. Paris is awfully expensive, and the job was very competitive. We hardly saw one another for three years. So much for the romance of Parisian life!" Ruth didn't mention the developing problem of Marie Ange, the pretty secretary. "But Jakarta is a promotion for him and a good chance to work in a developing country. I don't know what I think yet— I've never been in Asia before!"

"Any plans to get involved in charity work or fundraising for pet projects here? The leper colony gets you lots of points with the powers-that-be!" Ruth had been through this in other posts; it was the standard new colleague quiz.

"Leper colony? Not sure I would be up for that ...anything else I could do? I would like to get involved in something helpful, but I need to find my feet first. My sister was killed last winter, and I am still finding my way without her."

"Oh, I'm so sorry about your sister! What a terrible loss!"

"Thank you. We were close -- she was my "big sister", my leader in everything. She was a dancer, and I hope to learn something of the dance culture in Indonesia -- it would be a way to stay close to her now. Perhaps there would be some way into that world and something I could do to be helpful -- fundraising, maybe?"

"I think there are a couple of wives who are involved with the Javanese dance group here -- Helke Ramsey for example. She might be helpful. And there's always tennis and bridge, and gossip of course. Lots of that around this year! Hmm — let's see — did I mention the feral cat rescue?" But then Gwen, leaning forward and lowering her voice confidentially, said something surprising — "I am going to be indiscreet and warn you right now to be careful. This place is a nest of vipers! The current ambassador has pretty much left, only shows up occasionally, and Congress doesn't approve of any of the names submitted to them and won't confirm anyone -- so competing factions here have a free hand to run the place, and the gossip is vicious. Don't trust anyone! "

Ruth was surprised -- such candor wasn't normal in her experience of foreign service posts--and didn't reply immediately and Gwen went on "also, there's quite a lot of discontent being stirred up by reports of demonstrations against the Vietnam war back home, and some wives are becoming quite outspoken about the lack of opportunities for women in the foreign service. And the department won't allow married women to serve as FSOs!"

"Oh, yes, a woman officer in Paris got married and had to resign!" Ruth said. "The "marriage rule"! Doesn't seem as though it will ever change."

Gwen tilted her head to the side and sighed gently, saying "I've never thought about these things before, and I honestly don't really know what to think. My husband thinks we shouldn't rock the boat though." As she finished, Ruth thought -- why, she looks like a blue jay, head cocked, bright eyes contemplating something new in the feeder, full of mischief and trouble.

Just then, a second car entered the driveway and another woman appeared at the door, this one with short gray hair, no make-up, wearing sensible shoes and carrying a bunch of daisies. If Gwen's a blue jay, this one's a sparrow, thought Ruth. Again, a servant whisked the flowers away as the newcomer introduced herself. "Hi, there! I'm Belinda Forrest. You met my husband Joe yesterday, and I wanted to drop by to say hello and see if you need anything. Our husbands are going to be departmental colleagues." Noticing Gwen, she hesitated for a moment and continued "Oh, Gwen! How nice of you to come by so quickly! I'd forgotten you live close." The slight coolness in the greeting and the hesitation beforehand piqued Ruth's interest. Maybe this sparrow's not so timid, tread carefully, she thought, remembering Gwen's so-recent warning.

Siti, a young woman with a sweet smile and a graceful manner, brought a tray of coffee and the conversation became general, with advice on household management, food shopping, local customs, all the everyday trivia needed in a new posting. Zoe wandered through to greet the guests, fixing her smoky blue eyes on each in turn, patting their knees with gentle paws, charming them. Ruth laughed — "She's being Madame Ambassador and trying to talk you into giving her some treats, don't fall for it."

"I'm going shopping later this week at Toko Sunlight, Ruth, if you would like to join me. I 'll let you know what day", Belinda offered and Gwen followed with an invitation to spend the afternoon at the swimming pool with her:

"It will give you a chance to relax, and to meet some of the local inhabitants," she said "and see how we "trailing spouses" entertain ourselves when we are off-duty and not being good little representatives of the United States of

America." Belinda looked uncomfortable at this faintly-critical remark, but said nothing.

As the guests stood to leave, Ruth accepted Gwen's invitation, saying "I would love to join you at the pool, Gwen", intending to use the chance to find out more about her feminist opinions and try to see whether or not she wanted to be a friend or was simply a troublemaker and gossip. Belinda extended a dinner invitation to Ruth and Mark for the following evening, pointedly excluding Gwen.

After they left, she decided to rest and started for the bedroom but before she could get there, there was a hullaballoo from the kitchen and rear courtyard, and Zoe streaked through the room with her fur and tail bushed out, disappearing under the nearest sofa. Ruth ran to the kitchen and was met by the women servants talking excitedly and gesturing toward the courtyard where she could see Suleiman glaring angrily around at the crowd and shouting something in Indonesian. Point down in the grass a few feet away from him was his knife, still quivering from the force with which it had struck the ground,

Chapter Three

Suleiman is Dismissed

YaYa, the cook from next door, had been alerted by the din and haltingly explained to Ruth that Suleiman had thrown his knife at Zoe, missing her by a whisker. According to YaYa, Suleiman resented the cat and had decided that he would drive her away or injure her so badly that she would die. "What was he shouting, YaYa?" Ruth asked.

"Say he no like cat" answered YaYa, looking down at the ground and not at Ruth. She, wondering what little Zoe could have done and, utterly at a loss as to how to deal with this bizarre situation, told Suleiman to go to the servants' quarters and wait for Mark to come home. Zoe was apparently unhurt, and she was safe under the sofa. Perhaps she should fire Suleiman right now to demonstrate that she was in charge of the household. Not completely sure of the position of women in this new culture, she didn't feel comfortable doing that yet but it would be a relief, she thought, to not see the cook moodily stropping that knife.

Remembering her date with Gwen, she dialed Gwen's number and, miraculously, the phone worked. "Gwen" she began, "I've got a situation here and I need to stay and work things out. Can we go to the pool another time?"

After she sketched the story, Gwen asked "Would it help if I came over? I could translate a bit, and you might feel better with some support."

"Oh, yes! That would be great! Please come! I don't want to bother Mark on his first day at the office but I just don't know what to do! And perhaps you can help me understand the staff situation too."

Gwen arrived on foot a few minutes later, flushed and sticky, saying "It's *siang*, siesta time. Too hot to be out. My driver was asleep, so I walked. Water and shade, please!"

After hearing the full story, interrupted by a few tears from Ruth, Gwen advised her "You can talk to the admin office about the staff. Usually, they hire a temporary staff for new arrivals, selected from a list kept by them. Sometimes the new family keeps those people on, but they don't have to."

"How do they select the people?" asked Ruth "do they check references?"

"Well, usually the people on the list have worked for expat families previously, or they are family members that they bring in. You don't see written references often, mostly it's word of mouth, because so many people are illiterate; written ones are treasured, and their paper is often worn soft and hardly legible because they've been handled so much."

"Do the servants have keys to the house?" asked Ruth.

Gwen replied "Not usually, except to the back door that leads to the rear courtyard where the staff rooms are. The cook or whoever is in charge will have that key so that he or she can lock up at night and open early in the morning."

"I think I will ask Mark to check with the admin office about Suleiman's references. I noticed this morning that the other servants don't seem to like him very much—there's no friendly chatter when he's around, and they are all very formal and quiet, which makes me wonder about him."

Thinking for a moment about what Gwen had said about written references and illiteracy, Ruth said "Oh, Suleiman seems to be literate. This morning I gave him a written list for the market, and he didn't ask for any help with it. Is that odd?"

"Yes, a little. My driver can read a bit, but none of the other servants can. That's another favorite project for spouses here—literacy. So, what do you want to do about Suleiman anyway?"

After a short conference, they decided that Ruth would dismiss the cook. Together, they marched out to the rear courtyard and summoned him to the back door, where Gwen, interpreting, told him that his services were no longer needed, and requested his key to the house. Ruth handed him a small sum of money and he left without argument, although scowling and obviously angry as he went out the gate, the big handle of his knife sticking out of his bag.

"A new experience every day in the foreign service!" said Ruth, as they turned to re-enter the house. "That man scares me. I hope he doesn't come back, holding a grudge along with his knife." The women servants had assembled at the door behind them, now smiling and all talking at once. It appeared that they too had been afraid of

Suleiman and his knife. "So" asked Ruth "how did he get hired, Gwen? I told you the others didn't like him."

About 4 o'clock, Mark arrived home, and Zoe emerged unhurt from the sofa's depths. The heat of the day was subsiding and the shady screened porch with its fans and big rattan chairs was a pleasant place to sit and talk over the day's events. Ruth ran through her list — Suleiman and his knife, Gwen's helping her to translate, and their joint dismissal of Suleiman, and said that she felt she and Gwen could be friends.

Mark responded "hmm, yeah, I heard some things today that made me think about what she said to you yesterday about gossip and factions. There were some broad hints about the admin officer and his assistant; she's a young pretty Indonesian, he's a married man, and people implied that they are having an affair. The Suleiman thing could have something to do with that — perhaps she's a relative of his and she got him the job."

Ruth laughed. "That sounds about right. I bet jobs with foreigners are pretty sought-after—well-paid by local standards, lots of extras like access to foreign stuff, regular income, and not too demanding. And speaking of servants, let's see what the cook has made for dinner." As they headed to the dining porch, Ruth suddenly said "I wonder ... how much money would be in something like that? I mean, an under-cover job agency and influence peddling operation? Not much if it were just for servants, but what about people with more money? Positions with international agencies, inside tips on contracts, whose palm would accept grease? Maybe an occasional visa application given special approval?"

Mark stopped and turned to look at her. "Odd that you should say that. Someone today was joking about the admin office having a deal on those palms that they give to new arrivals, saying that the embassy must the sole support of the supplier because his prices are outlandish. You can buy the same palms in the bazaar for half the price he charges the embassy. Maybe the admin office has other deals that make a lot more money than a potted palm.

"Oh, and I almost forgot— Gwen was right about the ambassador too. Congress doesn't seem to be able to agree on a nominee and still hasn't confirmed anyone. Things here are out of control. There are competing factions and a lot of gossip. Apparently, our friend Joe is up to his neck in the intrigue!"

"Wow! That's quite a rundown!" said Ruth "let's eat and think about it!" Dinner was simple, served at the table in the dining porch; red snapper with a peanut sauce, rice, and a salad which tasted faintly of the chlorine solution used to disinfect the leaves.

"Perhaps we'll get used to it, then bore everyone to death with our gourmet recollections," said Mark, "ah, yes, 1968 chlorine was the best by far ...the delicate taste, the subtle aroma, and the slight tang—." But there was a nice bottle of wine which someone had thoughtfully put in the refrigerator to chill, and they relaxed, beginning to be comfortable as their bodies adjusted to the heat. Ruth started to think of ways to make the house more their own, but realized that it would take some work and imagination to liven up the modern furniture supplied to every foreign service officer around the world. Anyway, their own stuff would help a lot, but it was still on the high seas in a container, and might show up in a month. Or a year.

Darkness came suddenly, without twilight. They listened to the night noises for a while: the sounds of the food vendors passing by in the street - a small gong for the satay man with his charcoal grill, a clicker for the snack seller, a bamboo flute for the corn fritter man and inside the house, the loud clicking KkkkkkK of the small translucent pink geckos that lived behind the pictures and curtains of the unairconditioned rooms. Spicy food smells wafted in, along with the fragrant smoke of *kretek*, clove cigarettes sold singly by the *kretek* vendor from his little stall under the tree on the corner. The tropical night was sensual, warm and enfolding, reminding them that they were still young. And, thought Ruth, Marie Ange was safely 7,000 miles away in Paris. Time for bed.

Chapter Four

1968
Eleanor Calls

"Mark, don't forget we are going to dinner with Joe and Belinda tonight" Ruth said as they breakfasted in the dining porch early the next day.

"Oh damn, I forgot" replied Mark "must we? I saw enough of that bore during the day in the office, let alone spending an evening listening to him bloviate about how successful he is in his career. Which he isn't -- he's incompetent and lazy."

"Well, I understand, but at least it will be an opportunity to meet other staff members, and get a feeling for morale," Ruth said, attempting to smooth things, "and maybe the food will be good."

The prospect of a couple of hours at dinner with the overbearing Belinda and the loquacious Joe was daunting; she hoped at least the other guests would be interesting. But during the day she wanted to be a tourist and explore this new city, and wondered if Gwen could join her. It would be a good chance to learn more about Gwen too — I need an ally to guide me through this mysterious and charged landscape, she thought.

Their car hadn't arrived yet, and the telephone didn't work today. The servants had told Gwen yesterday that this was a good house, Ruth recalled, because there were only a couple of resident *hantu*--spirits, and they were not difficult or mischievous. But the resident spirits apparently controlled the telephone and the water pump, and who knew what else, thought Ruth. No voices were magicked into the black machine by them this morning. Were the offerings adequate? Did the *hantu* of the telephone require something different from the *hantu* of the water pump? Gwen said the servants had been clear that she of the water pump required white rice in a ceramic bowl, to keep her pumping water from the underground cistern into the house, so they provided it fresh every morning. Perhaps *hantu telopon* needs rose petals or gardenias, instead of plain white rice? Black rice in a silver bowl? A hardboiled egg occasionally? She needed to consult Siti and Muriarti, the authorities on the house's spirits, but meanwhile — how to reach Gwen?

The diplomatic list left on the desk with the post report supplied the address, so she wrote a quick note and gave it to Siti, sending her down the street to deliver it while she showered and dressed in something cool, pulling her blond hair back into a loose chignon and hoping that the clothes she had chosen so carefully in Paris were appropriate for life in a tropical Muslim country. Would the current mini-skirt fashion be a problem? It did make bending down difficult, requiring a sideways bend to maintain modesty and decorum but certainly showed off pretty tanned legs. Well, she thought, these batik fabrics that I see on all the servants are very attractive and there must be dressmakers, if necessary.

As she waited for a reply from Gwen, she thought about the responsibilities that she would have in the next few days. After tonight's introduction to Mark's colleagues, she would be expected to make formal calls on the wives of senior embassy officials, and leave the appropriate number of engraved cards with the correct corners turned down, the right "code" written in initials on them, and stay for the regulation ten minutes, no more, no less. "P.f.c" would be appropriate for most of them — French for "*pour faire connaisance*", meaning "to make your acquaintance." While it was dated, there was something to be said for meeting the wives of the upper echelon of the embassy staff so that you could recognize them, and also so they could be sure you knew your place in the spousal pecking order.

She heard a car in the driveway and a voice called out "Hello, there! Anybody home?" as the door to the living room opened. Really, thought Ruth, doesn't anyone use the doorbell around here? The woman who entered carried no flowers, but was the single most beautiful woman Ruth had ever seen. Tall, slim, with long glossy black hair, a creamy complexion and dark blue eyes surrounded by thick black lashes — "put in with a sooty finger" Ruth's grandmother had said about such eyes. "I'm Eleanor Jackson" said this apparition, "I manage the embassy grocery store, and I was passing on the way to open up for the day and decided to stop and say Hi, welcome, hope you'll be happy here, and that we'll have everything you need!"

Noticing the palm from the admin office, she continued "Oh, I am so glad this got to you! We had some problems getting these from the merchant last week, so I am pleased yours got here. But this one doesn't look very healthy, and it isn't really a good plant. I will have it replaced for you."

Hoisting the pot, she trotted out, palm fronds gracefully waving a green goodbye over her elegant shoulder. "Bye-bye!"

Ruth, seeking a tiny flaw in this perfection, thought Eleanor a little over made-up and overdressed for a weekday morning on her way to work, and the whole situation very odd. A commonplace palm, nothing unusual about it, and just to pick it up and remove it without asking Ruth's permission? Why would Eleanor notice it? In fact, why would Eleanor stop in to meet her? She manages the commissary, she meets everyone eventually and doesn't need to go out of her way to say welcome. Bizarre.

Gwen arrived as Eleanor drove off in her sporty Mercedes with a man riding beside her in the front seat. Gwen rushed in (without ringing the bell. Ruth made a mental note to check whether the bell worked) and said "What on earth? What was Eleanor doing here? Ruth, I hope you didn't say ANYTHING to that toxic gossip! She really enjoys stirring things up, then sitting back to watch the result! Not that she's got any room to talk—did you see her boyfriend sitting in the car?"

"I have no idea what she wanted, Gwen. She said she just dropped in on her way to the commissary, then she took that potted palm that was left for us yesterday! What is it with these palms? She said it wasn't a 'good plant' and that she would replace it...I don't understand why it matters. She has a boyfriend, and he was in the front seat? I thought he was her driver!"

Gwen sighed. Evidently it was time to acquaint Ruth with the facts of life in expatriate circles in Jakarta. "That was her boyfriend, not her driver. Eleanor is married to a foreign service officer, a consular officer. He apparently doesn't earn enough money to keep her in the style she likes, so she got herself the job managing the embassy commissary. It doesn't pay a lot —I'm on the commissary board, so I know what she makes— but I guess with what she gets from him, it's enough." Pausing for a moment, she gave a mocking laugh, a derisive birdlike cackle "She dresses expensively—a bit flashy though, kind of successful California hairdresser style—and she's been spotted with the boyfriend once or twice at those illegal high roller Chinese gambling palaces down in Kota Baru."

"And the ugly potted palms? Why does everyone get one when they arrive? Does Eleanor get a cut from the potted palm merchant, to cover her mahjong addiction? Or does she prefer the roulette wheel?" Ruth, on a roll now, continued "Why did she stop here? I am sure it wasn't because she wanted to meet me, she can do that when I go in to get groceries. And the boyfriend—does her husband know?"

There was a long pause—an angel passing perhaps, as the French say when there is a lag in conversation—while Ruth waited for answers, and Gwen, although usually ready for a good long gossip, wondered how much more to say. "So many questions! So little time!" she said at last.

Ruth waited for more, but nothing came. Eventually she said "I need to go to the embassy to set up our commissary account, and ask about the servants' references. Would you like to come with me and join me for lunch afterwards?"

"Yes, that would be fun! My car's outside. I'm sure my driver's gossiping in the courtyard with your lot—getting material for the local grapevine! They're probably telling him about Suleiman's firing, with flourishes! The whole town will know about it tomorrow, and we'll be heroines!"

Chapter Five

The Admin Section

In the car, driven by Gwen's driver, Ruth came back to the question of "the boyfriend" "Who is he? Does Eleanor's husband know about him? How does this kind of thing go down with the ambassador and the expat community?"

"Well, it looks like a long-term arrangement. He's been around for a year or so, I think. His name's Florin Radu — Romanian, some kind of entrepreneur — lots of them around these days, looking to make a buck off Vietnam. I don't know whether her husband knows, although he probably does. There are a lot of people who would relish spreading choice gossip like this, especially where Eleanor is concerned -- she's not popular."

Gwen paused for a moment, reflecting: "There's no ambassador right now, and community opinion? Most of the foreign community are sophisticated enough to pretend they aren't interested in stuff like this, but they enjoy some gossip on the side. A bit of spice keeps morale high, if not morals! And the servants' grapevine is a tropical plant growing like a beanstalk in the expat soil here, spreading the news at the speed of light."

Ruth giggled, then said "Wow! So how do I tune in to this grapevine?"

"You hang around the kitchen. Your own cook, Muriarti, is a great source -- she knows all about everyone! You need some language classes though, so sign up. State

Department pays for language classes for families, but you know that from your other posts. Life's pretty dull here, really. We're mostly civil servants of one kind or another, US, Australian, international. We don't have any gossip mags and we gotta get our jollies somehow, plus things are pretty loose in the tropics and there's usually something mildly sensational going on. Best not to get mentioned too much though!"

To Ruth, this seemed like a good opportunity to ask Gwen about Paul Faber's disappearance. "Mark was told in Washington about the accident— that's why he was assigned here, to fill Paul's vacant place—but he didn't get much more than a bare outline. What's the real story, is there more to know?"

Gwen sighed and began reluctantly "I wondered when you would ask" but, warming to the task, she continued eagerly "It's all pretty murky, and there's been a lot of gossip about it. A group — all men—had been drinking heavily — Bintang Baru beer with whiskey chasers —and they shouldn't have gone swimming at all, especially at such a notoriously dangerous place. There are sudden drop-offs and strong rip currents at high tide; the hotel has warning signs around, and people have drowned there in the past. The speculation is wild — taken by a shark is probably the least colorful! Grabbed by someone and held under the water is another--why? Or just a routine drowning accident—it's happened down there more than once. The Indonesian authorities investigated, but since they couldn't find Paul's body, they couldn't really close the case. And the State Department security people weren't terribly helpful for some reason.

"How old was he? I got the impression he was pretty young to be Counselor of Embassy. Did he have a family?"

Gwen was enjoying herself now, talking fast and gesturing expressively -- "Oh, he was a young healthy guy, and a good swimmer, so it wouldn't have been easy to hold him down, if that's what happened. And wouldn't others have noticed the commotion? And why would someone want to kill him? No-one has come up with a convincing reason so far. He was a single guy, well-liked, popular with women but didn't seem to have anyone special — not that there weren't some who were circling. And yes, there was a bit of gossip about high-level connections getting him his job. People said he wasn't really qualified. Had an uncle who is a senator, maybe strings got pulled."

"Thanks for telling me. I can see there's a lot to think about, since Mark's rather directly involved, being sent in as his replacement. Let's talk again later. I don't even know what questions to ask yet."

They were quiet for a while, the car moving along a four-lane highway leading to the city, passing cramped houses built of brick and stucco with red tile roofs like the one on Ruth's house, small shops, and large open areas where people were making furniture and offering it for sale to passersby. Ruth was attracted by a group of large birdcages made of wood and wire, topped with Indonesian carving painted red, blue and gold.

"They're really pretty, aren't they?" said Gwen, noticing Ruth's attentive gaze " A lot of people put them outside the front door sheltered under the eaves, and fill them with a little flock of parakeets. Be charming outside your dining porch, where you could see and hear the birds."

Ruth decided to order one, as a first step in making their new house into their home, and Gwen bargained with the owner for a while on her behalf. Concluding the deal, she said "We probably paid too much — foreigners, having a car, etc., but it's pretty cheap anyway. I promise you that someone with a dozen budgies will show up at your door within fifteen minutes of its arrival! Everything comes to the door, you just watch!"

George Stewart, the administrative officer, a man with a confident smile and a slight swagger, was available. He held Ruth's hand a bit too long after their handshake, squeezing it gently before releasing it and saying warmly "I am glad to meet you, Ruth! I'll be glad to help you any way I can." He couldn't though tell them much about Suleiman and his employment. "Yeah, he's known around here, worked for a couple of expat families with no complaints as far as we know. His most recent employers have left Jakarta, and I don't know where they went — they weren't embassy people." Ruth asked if he had a record of who had referred Suleiman to the embassy this time, "No, no record of that. But I'll ask Vicky Ormond, my deputy, if she knows anything more."

Not a very satisfying interview, thought Ruth. Was Stewart being evasive? And if he was having an affair with his assistant, could the assistant have slipped Suleiman's name onto the list? And why? The most obvious answer, of course, would be a favor, perhaps to a family member or close friend, or maybe a bribe. For services rendered, or as a down payment on future help?

As they left the administrative office, Eleanor arrived, swanning in confidently, giving them a wide, patronizing smile. The door of George Stewart's office closed behind her with a decisive click, leaving them dismissed, interlopers in weighty affairs. Gwen, in a low mutter, said "Big decision day, I guess. She probably has to negotiate a rush order on sleds and snowshoes for next winter. Or maybe the palms aren't making any money."

Seeing Eleanor again reminded Ruth of something. "Gwen, I've been thinking about that palm that Eleanor took from my house -- I think she came just to get it and remove it. There isn't any other reason for that strange visit. Why on earth did she want it? Could it have anything to do with Suleiman's temper fit at Zoe?" She stopped, realizing that this wasn't really the place to discuss it, then said "Well, we can't talk about it here! Where shall we go for lunch? Iis there some place close by where we could take our unimportant selves?"

"Yes, there's a lovely Balinese place nearby. We won't run into Eleanor or her cronies there either — she doesn't like Indonesian food. I don't know why she even stays here! No interest in her husband, leaves her kids to be taken care of by the servants, and doesn't like the country. Must be something that keeps her here, though."

Chapter Six

Lunch with the Goddess Melanting

To reach the outer world, Gwen and Ruth made their way past a series of pools and fountains in a formal courtyard which presented an image of order and unity, contrasting strongly with the apparently anarchic energy of the people and vehicles in the streets outside. Three years after a bloody uprising and change of government in Indonesia, security at the US Embassy was strong but discreet, the iron fist hidden by a velvet glove. Imposing, costly, and carefully designed to demonstrate the power and strength of the United States, the embassy grounds needed no show of arms to make the point.

Once outside the gates, Gwen and Ruth's walk from the embassy took them down a shady street to a small restaurant in a garden, with a sign saying "Makan Dewi Melanting." The path leading to the open front door was covered by a blue-purple pool of fallen blossoms from the jacaranda tree in the garden, and a tall birdcage stood under the eaves of the porch, in just the way Gwen had described that morning. Ruth exclaimed "Oh, Gwen! That's lovely — I hope mine will look as good at my house! I've never had a tropical garden, and it's glorious. I need to know where to buy plants and start filling in the space around my house too!"

Gwen laughed "The name of the restaurant means "Food of the Goddess Melanting" — she's the Balinese goddess of gardens and markets! There are some beautiful gardens here — the soil is so rich that you stick a plant in and get out of the way as it shoots up. I heard a story about someone in the embassy who planted tomatoes, with bamboo stakes to hold them up. The tomato plants died of the heat, but the bamboo stakes grew!"

A small bronze gong stood on a carved chest in the front hall; Gwen struck it gently and a barefoot woman servant wearing traditional Indonesian dress appeared silently from somewhere in the rear of the house. She indicated with a hand that they should follow her and led them through a wide doorway and a trellised porch covered with a fragrant jasmine vine, into a flowery space dappled with sun and shadow.

In the aqueous light under the lush foliage of flowering trees were a number of small tables set with attractive linens, where guests—mostly women— were seated. They were a cosmopolitan group—Indonesian ladies in crisp *kain* and lacy *kebaya* with silk scarves laid lightly over their hair in the Muslim style, Indians in *saris* or casual *salwar kameez*, Europeans and Americans in short linen shift dresses with puffy Filipino embroidered sleeves or simple dresses in dramatic batik fabrics. There were Chinese ladies too, in tailored *cheongsam*, and a few men in tropical business attire. Discreet jewelry, expensively-sandaled feet, manicured hands and attentive grooming, they were in every way a representation of the upper-middle-class to which they belonged — or hoped to belong. Faintly, Ruth could hear in the background of the feminine chatter the rippling music of an orchestra of small gongs, and recognized it from recordings as a Javanese gamelan.

A young woman called out to Gwen and asked them to join her group. "Would you mind, Ruth? She's a good friend." Ruth agreed, and they made their way to the table. Gwen introduced her friend to Ruth quickly — "Ruth, my friend Charlotte. Charlotte, Ruth" and the others at the table introduced themselves casually — Solange, the wife of a French diplomat, and Margaret, a consular officer at the US Embassy, while Charlotte, also at the US Embassy, was a political officer who worked with Gwen's husband.

"Ruth and her husband Mark have just arrived. Mark is the new economic counselor, replacing Paul Faber. They have that new house on Jalan Widjaya."

"Welcome, Ruth," said Charlotte. "I hope you will like Jakarta. That's a nice house! Your husband has certainly walked into a tricky situation, hasn't he? The rumors have been lurid! I've heard speculation that Paul was snatched by the Viet Cong for ransom at some future time, or that Nyi Loro Kidul, the sea goddess, snatched him because she wanted something new in her room in the hotel, or … Your husband have anything new to add?"

Ruth, feeling ambushed by the question and slightly defensive, laughed politely. "No new information, not to my knowledge anyway. But — tell me about the Sea Goddess! She sounds a bit autocratic, snatching bureaucrats for private use!"

"Oh, the hotel down there at Samudra Beach where Paul disappeared was built by President Sukarno, in the sixties" began Solange "He was the first president of Indonesia, and he loved pretty women—he had five wives, not all at once though! — and claimed to have met Nyi Loro Kidul herself on the beach there. To please her, he built a hotel..."

Margaret broke in "He thought it would be good for the infant Indonesian tourist trade too, so not entirely impractical."

"Ah, you unromantic Americans!" said Solange, then continued: "Room 308 is still reserved for her; it's the room with the best view of the ocean, and it's kept filled with flowers, candles, offerings, and paintings supposed to be of Nyi Loro herself. It's a shrine, and for a few rupiahs, you can visit it when you're down there. Perhaps she wanted new company... Paul was an interesting man, I believe he was from a French family, you know-- and women liked him, although he seemed indifferent to them."

"Yes, he was very attractive, and fun too!" Margaret interjected, "a lot of women here noticed that and made a bit of a play for him, but no-one had much luck, other than a date for some official function or other when he needed an escort, I suppose. A pity, really. Probably wouldn't have been interested in Nyi Loro!"

Menus arrived, handwritten in English and Indonesian on heavy paper backed with exotic fabric, and Ruth received a great deal of advice about what she should choose. "Don't drink the water" said Solange "wine is safer ... and better, as long as it's French." Ruth, under Solange's supervision, chose a corn and shrimp pancake and a glass of wine. As they gave their orders to the young woman who had met them at the door, the conversation in the garden suddenly dwindled to a low murmur. Gwen nudged Ruth, and called her attention to a couple who had just entered.

The man was forty-ish, tall and athletic-looking although not especially handsome, and dressed in well-tailored casual clothes. He was holding the arm of his companion, a striking woman no longer in her first youth but still beautiful. Tiny, with erect carriage, her long dark hair was drawn back to show high cheekbones and dramatically made-up eyes. Her black silk dress contrasted strongly with the casually expensive and colorful cottons and linens worn by the other women in the garden, its long flowing skirt giving it a timeless grace lacking in the miniskirted styles of the day. A heavy necklace of amber and gold beads was her only jewelry, and she carried nothing in her hand but a fan made of batik with gilded bamboo ribs.

The hostess showed them to a table near the edge of the seating area, slightly screened by an enthusiastically-flourishing hibiscus bush and out of earshot of the other guests. They began a whispered conversation, heads close together, apparently completely unaware of the shocked looks passing around the garden.

"Alright, everyone" said Ruth into the strained silence at her table "who are they, and why does everyone look like they've seen a ghost?"

Solange, appearing stunned but trying to recover, said "Oh la la, that's Nina Petrovna, the wife of the Soviet ambassador... are they holding hands?" as Gwen hissed "that's Eleanor's husband!"

Chapter Seven

The Ride Home from Lunch

The food and wine were delicious, but the chatter was guarded. No-one — at their table, anyway —wanted to comment too openly on what had just happened, and people rushed through their lunches. Solange asked if she could get a lift home in Gwen's car, saying she had sent her driver off to pick up her daughter at school, so the conversation in the car was stilted at first although they were all three dying to discuss the events at the restaurant.

At last Ruth could wait no longer, "That dress! And the amber necklace! Theatrical, but stunning! The outfit made me want to go home and throw away all my clothes and start over!"

Solange said "I met Nina Petrovna a few times, you know—she was a first soloist on her way up the ladder to principal dancer at the Kirov — the Maryiinsky — in Leningrad, until she left a couple of years ago to marry Ambassador Smirnov."

"You know her?" said Gwen, surprised. "The Soviet Embassy people don't mix much with the rest of the diplomatic group."

"Well, I can't say I know her well, but I met her a few times in a dance class that she used to have at the residence. I suppose she wanted an opportunity to exercise and maintain some of her skill. No-one ever had much of a chance to chat with her though. Someone always came in to escort her out of the room when we finished the class."

"How did you get included in the class?" asked Ruth, remembering how closely held the classes at the Bolshoi were during her years in Moscow. "All the embassy women were dying to have an opportunity to take classes with the professionals, but it was just not permitted."

"I think the invitation came to the ambassador —we French still try to maintain a cordial relationship with the Soviets— and a couple of us who had ballet experience were sent over. It was very difficult, way above my level. There was a pianist, and a Gorgon of a ballet mistress -- *tiens!* so strict! --they must have come from the Soviet Union with the ambassador, and it was a completely professional class. She was exquisite to watch, but I never thought she was happy. Such an air of reserve and ... melancholy. Smirnov is a lot older than she — perhaps she is regretting her marriage."

"What makes you say that? Anything in particular?" Gwen asked.

Solange thought for a moment, then decided to continue "Well, I probably shouldn't mention this, but I was reminded of it when I saw her at lunch today. I was having lunch up at Bogor one day with a Dutch friend, at the little restaurant in the old Dutch Governor General's residence and I saw her with a man I later learned was Paul Faber. It was an odd little thing — hardly anybody knows about that restaurant, and it's more than 30 miles away from Jakarta.

"My friend Marieke and I like to visit the Bogor Botanic Gardens — enormous trees, orchids growing in the branches, glorious. We've never seen any other diplomats there, and we decided to keep quiet about seeing them because it was strange and perhaps significant somehow."

Ruth and Gwen were silent, trying to process this development. After the discussion at lunch of Paul Faber's lack of interest in any of the women in his orbit in Jakarta, this required thought. And amazed respect for Solange and her friend Marieke, both of whom had resisted the opportunity to pass on some sensational gossip!

At last, Ruth said tentatively "So. Two American diplomats seen separately lunching *à deux* with the exquisite Madame Smirnova. the Soviet ambassador's wife? In the middle of the cold war, Vietnam in flames, the US close to rebellion— one a secret lunch in a secluded place, the other with Eleanor's husband, holding hands and lunching in front of a large part of the expat community. Did I put that right?"

"Well, to be fair" ... said Gwen "they weren't really holding hands, maybe just touching, but yes. And now I am remembering the hints and sly insinuations about Paul Faber — that he was gay, and that's why he wasn't interested in any of the women here. Perhaps he was in love with Nina Petrovna, and that's why he wasn't interested."

Solange sighed, and said, "it was such a romantic scene, that lunch! This very beautiful woman, so elegantly dressed and coiffed, the handsome man, lunching together in a simple restaurant, the world a million miles away for them. They were completely absorbed in one another. Of course, the food wasn't terribly good (it isn't French, you know), but I suppose it wasn't important to them because they had each other."

Gwen continued, "But Paul's gone now. He was a single man, Bernie's married. Nina Petrovna is a very attractive woman — could this be a high-level honey trap? Looking for secret information, and maybe the plan had to be revised when Paul disappeared? Eleanor doesn't pay Bernie any attention — she has other fish to fry; but I don't think he has much access to classified information — he's a consular officer, restricted to issuing visas and renewing passports."

Sighing slightly, Solange said "Truly, you Americans have no romance in your souls! A love affair between such beautiful people should be treasured, not discussed like a purchase at the *fromagerie*!"

Ruth ignored her — "Visas to the USA are valuable, Gwen! And passports even more so! The consulate safe is probably full of passport blanks—I wonder how much one of those would be worth to someone caught in the aftermath of the uprisings here."

"Well, visa-selling is certainly an old and distinguished tradition in the foreign service!" Gwen replied. "We all heard those stories in junior officer training! Passport blanks though — I hadn't thought of that possibility, but it would require a lot of teamwork. The passport numbers are carefully recorded, and if one were to disappear, it would immediately be reported to the authorities."

"Unless ... it was an inside job. Someone with control of the blanks and the list of numbers" said Ruth "...take one out of the middle, it might not be missed for months."

Exasperated with them, Solange said "Truly, *c'est vrai*, what they say about Americans! They have the souls of grocers! Here's my street — you can drop me here, and I'll walk the rest of the way. Thanks for the ride."

With Solange gone, Ruth and Gwen felt free to be even less discreet. Gwen didn't want to relinquish the romantic possibility yet: "She could certainly do better than Bernie Jackson though. There was a story on the grapevine recently about her toothsome Brazilian tennis coach. Those Brazilians certainly play a lively game!"

"Oh, for heaven's sake, Gwen! It's not funny! What are we going to think of next ... that our ambassador's wife is smuggling gold, and that Eleanor has a ruinous gambling addiction that she indulges in the illegal Chinese gambling palaces down in the old town? Let's go home. I need some time to rest before I have to go to the Forrests' for dinner. And who knows? Maybe President of the International School PTA or Belinda's other do-gooding is a cover for her human trafficking activities and all will be revealed soon." Ruth flounced a little and turned her gaze to the road along which they were riding.

Gwen said, in a quiet voice "I know it sounds silly and a bit hysterical. Something is going on here. Rob and I are convinced that some of the embassy staff are involved in something illegal or unethical. Just can't figure it out yet. But keep watching, and you will see more odd things going on."

They rode home in silence, speaking again only when they arrived at Ruth's door, a bit reserved after their little tiff. But then Gwen saw, under the roof overhang, the birdcage. "Look, Ruth! It's here already, and all set up with everything but the birds!" Large, colorful, it snuggled into its space as if it were meant to live there, its stick perches and china food bowls offering comfort for its future inhabitants.

"Oh!", cried Ruth "how exotic! Thank you for helping me buy this!" And even more exotic, a *tukang*, a vendor, sat by the door with his shoulder pole resting beside him, a cage at each end filled with softly-colored fluttering birds — blue, green, yellow, white, chattering quietly among themselves.

"Told you so", said Gwen, smiling. "The servants will know how much to pay the *tukang*. They'll take a little cut, but it won't be too bad." She got back into her car and departed, leaving Ruth dazedly trying to adjust to this world where such delightful things came to the door almost unbidden.

The servants were on the watch for her return, and came out to help with the choosing and bargaining. With the help of Siti the maid, Muriarti the cook, the advice of the *tukang*, and a great deal of sign language and miming, together they selected a dozen birds of mixed colors, and installed them in their new home. The birds quickly began to claim their spaces, to form pairs and twitter cheerfully, and Ruth felt that this new possession was a good omen. Zoe, always curious about household activity, had already arrived in front of the cage and appeared to approve of this diversion, intently watching the birds, shaking with excitement and occasionally chattering her teeth and growling.

Now for a rest and a shower, thought Ruth, as she picked up the reluctant and struggling Zoe and retreated to the air -conditioned bedroom to prepare to go to the Forrests' dinner. The day had already provided enough drama and excitement, and she fervently hoped the dinner would be as dull and pedestrian as she expected.

Chapter Eight

Dinner at Belinda and Joe Forrest's House

The ride to the Forrests' dinner was pleasantly quiet, with a soft breeze from the forward movement of the bicycle rickshaw known locally as a *betjak* and only the creaks and whirring of the wheels to break the silence. And Mark's grumbling, of course — "I wish we weren't going! I just don't like the man and from what you have said, I am not going to like his wife either."

"I think it will be interesting to meet other members of the embassy staff. They can't all be awful. There must be some congenial people here." Ruth responded, thinking to herself that he's in the mood to dislike everyone he meets tonight! I wonder why he's so cranky. In a moment, she got her answer.

"A bit of news at work," Paul said "a foreign service inspection team arrived unexpectedly today. Everyone's wondering what's going on — maybe Gwen and her husband were right about that. Must be something serious; first time I ever heard of a surprise inspection They're usually announced in plenty of time for everyone to clean up their old sloppy ways."

The double seat of the *betjak* was narrow, built for tiny Indonesians and snug for Mark and Ruth. The driver, perched behind and high above the passengers, pedaled silently. It was pleasant but also strange and unsettling to be propelled solely by the strength and energy of another human being, and Ruth silently resolved not to use the rickshaws in future if there were any other choice of transport, especially not with Mark in his current mood. No point in being snuggled together when he's so grumpy, she thought.

When they arrived at the Forrests' house, there were already several cars parked in the driveway, with their drivers lounging nearby smoking and chatting. The door was open, and the Fairchilds entered the house without ringing (no doorbell use here either). "Mark! Ruth! Good to see you! Hope you are settling in well" from Joe, with a hearty and sweaty handshake for Mark, and warm sticky hug for Ruth, one of his hands slightly too low for her comfort. "How nice to meet you at last, Mark! And Ruth, you look well", from Belinda, then they were free to mingle with Mark's new colleagues.

"Mind if I work the room, Ruth?", Mark said as he vanished into the crowd without waiting for her reply, leaving Ruth to observe her surroundings for a moment. The house was spacious, with the usual high ceilings and fans, and decorated with Indonesian art. Around her, she could hear shop talk, embassy gossip, stories about the eccentricities of servants, complaints about anything and everything — just like our last post, thought Ruth, as she smiled at everyone, and tried to pay attention to Belinda when she steamed up, a pocket battleship in a dowdy dress, to give Ruth instructions on making her calls. "Now tomorrow, here's a list for the driver, copy for you. My car will pick you up at 10 a.m. List's in order of precedence, top to bottom. Remember to stay no more than ten minutes at each house, this list tells you how many calling cards to leave, and don't forget to wear hose and a hat, and carry gloves."

Belinda's instructions were crisp, delivered with a schoolmistressly authority.

Ruth said "Oh, do I need to wear hose? They are so hot, and I only have one pair because I read in the post report that women don't use them here."

"Ruth, we have to maintain our standards, even if we are living in such a difficult place." Ah yes, thought Ruth, one must dress for dinner even in the jungle. Amused, she subsided. Maybe Gwen could tell her if she could safely ignore this nonsense. Who was going to check anyway? And would someone write in the section which reviewed the conduct of spouses in Mark's performance appraisal that she was not cooperative and wasn't a suitable representative of the United States government because she wouldn't wear panty hose in the tropics? I wouldn't mind being reviewed and judged, she thought, if I were paid but I'm not. I'm a "trailing spouse" -- charming description!

A servant announced that dinner was ready, and everyone moved to the dining room where a buffet meal was set out on a long dark wood table which appeared to be of Chinese design. There was a large Chinese bowl containing steaming aromatic chicken broth, then smaller serving bowls presenting noodles, small pieces of chicken, sliced cabbage and other green vegetables, ginger, quartered hardboiled eggs, and an array of spices, herbs, and sambals.

Belinda hovered, helping guests and sending servants to replenish items. She showed Ruth how to compose her own dinner in an individual bowl, and a pretty young woman joined Ruth as she moved down the line, introducing herself quickly as Helke Ramsey, wife of another member of the economic section staff. Helke made light chatter as they moved along "This is *soto ajam*— it's an Indonesian version of chicken soup, and Belinda's cook does it very well. Would you like to join my husband Howard and me to eat at one of those small tables over there?" Mark saw them and joined the little group, where he and fellow economist Howard Ramsey were soon deep in a lively discussion of South East Asian banking systems, Myrdal's theories of land reform, improved crop yields, and their applications to the wellbeing of the people of Indonesia, leaving Helke and Ruth to their own conversation.

Helke murmured discreetly to Ruth: "Economists do small talk so well, don't they? I saw you getting your assignments for your calls tomorrow. Don't worry — most of the women are nice and not as starchy as Belinda would have you think. And some of their houses are fabulous. It's actually pretty amusing, this whole antiquated calling thing."

"Must I wear stockings?" asked Ruth.

"What? Why would you do that?"

"Well, Belinda said I had to, or I'll break some golden rule about suitable clothing for dining in the jungle or something" Ruth said.

Helke began to laugh. "She tries that with all the new people. We think she wants us all to dress like she does. She buys her clothes from the Stylish Stout catalog, don't you think?"

Laughing, Ruth agreed— "Well, I shouldn't make quick judgments, but ..."

"She's very active in the foreign community, you know. Does a lot of good things — on the board of the swimming pool, PTA Chair at the International School, organizes activities at the American Women's Club. A real do-gooder. Since Paul Faber disappeared, she has been rather enjoying being spouse of the acting Chief of Section. Now that you're here, she might be a little disappointed that you are replacing her on that perch."

"Oh, lord!" exclaimed Ruth, "I don't want to be a Senior Wife! I just want to learn about the culture here, and help Mark as best I can. But thanks for telling me, so I can keep my eyes open." Belinda sounds like a real hazard, she thought — fingers in everything, a classic busybody.

"I hear you have one of the new houses" Helke continued "Be glad you didn't get the one that Paul had, over by the pool. He was our neighbor; the houses are way past their prime and the location is a problem. They back up to the swimming pool, and there are constant parties at night, lots of drinking, skinny-dipping, and strange traffic in the street. The pool's closed at night, of course, but all the houses have back gates into the pool compound. Paul wasn't happy about it, and Howie and I would like to move, but there isn't much housing choice at the moment." Helke paused, then said: "I also heard you fired Suleiman. He worked for Paul, you know. Not that you shouldn't have fired him, I just wondered if you knew that."

Ruth started to say "But George Stewart said ..." but broke off when Joe Forrest appeared in the dining room looking distressed, tapped on a glass to get attention, and announced "Belinda and I have to leave. I'm duty officer this week and there's been an incident at the embassy swimming pool that I need to deal with. Please stay and enjoy dinner. I don't know how long we will be gone."

Someone called out asking if he needed help. Joe hesitated for a moment before saying "The police are involved. A body was found floating in the pool an hour ago. That's all I know."

Chapter Nine

Day after Forrest Party

"Hi, honey! I'm home, and boy, am I wet" shouted Mark, as he ran in from the driveway, where a solid sheet of water cascaded, Niagara-loud, from a black sky. "I guess the monsoon has arrived."

Ruth and Siti were running from window to window closing them against the fierce onslaught, while Muriarti and Sunardi ran from the *godown*, the storeroom, bringing an assortment of buckets and pans to place under the leaks from the roof. "Glad you're home in one piece. I can't imagine what the road is like in this!" Ruth's voice could barely be heard over the pounding of the rain and the splashing of the leaks. "Do you think it does this every day in the rainy season? We're gonna need more buckets! I wondered why there were so many in the *godown,* and now I know!"

"What a day!" Paul shook himself as he headed for the bedroom; "Have I got a lot to tell you…it's been a doozy, beginning to end. Uh-oh …" as he opened the door of the bedroom. "Looks like we need some buckets in here too — the bed's wet, and the floor's a lake!"

As abruptly as it had started, the cataract stopped, leaving behind an eerie hush filled with the drip drip drip of the leaks from the ceiling, and the plaintive complaints of Zoe, marooned on the heights of the sofa back.

A couple of hours later, with house and people as dry as possible and Zoe liberated from her perch, Paul and Ruth settled on the screened porch, gin and tonics in hand. "Poor ZoZo! I think she'd rather still be a Parisian cat! I don't think I will ever complain again about the gray skies of Paris. So, what has been going on at the embassy that has given you such a doozy of a day?"

"Oof! Where to begin? The inspectors arrived, commandeered the ambassador's office suite, and started work."

"Anyone we know from other posts?" asked Ruth.

"No. In fact, these two aren't the usual kind of avuncular old-Joe's-reward-tour-before-retiring kind of inspector that we've met before. These are pretty hardnosed guys, young, a bit cold-eyed —seem more like FBI types than foreign service."

"Who are they talking to?"

"They seem to be starting with the lower levels — clerical staff, code people, admin—but not local employees, only US people— who must be getting stern warnings about talking, and their mouths are zipped shut! Nobody is uttering when they get through!"

Ruth replied "It might take a day or so for the fright to wear off, before they start to spill the beans. What do you think they're looking for?"

"Well, hard to know, but I am guessing something major. Serious security breach, major fiscal shenanigans, visa and citizenship stuff. Could be any or all of it." Mark held out his glass "Could I have a bit more ice, please, then I'll go on—there's plenty more I haven't told you yet."

"Just ice?"

"Yeah. Better keep a clear head tonight. Don't know if this is all over for the day."

Ruth fetched the ice, and Mark continued "And, of course, the body in the swimming pool is a major topic of interest! Not much leaking out about that either. George Stewart has been put in charge of it; he's working with the Indonesian police, and I guess Singapore will send somebody down to help him with the formalities."

"George Stewart? Really?" Surprised, Ruth jumped in "I told you that Helke Ramsey said that Suleiman — the cook with the knife—worked for Paul Faber. But the other day when I asked Stewart what he knew about him, he said he knew pretty much nothing, that Suleiman's former employers had left Jakarta and no-one knew where they went!"

"And" she continued "something else I haven't had time to tell you yet. I heard from someone when I was making my calls today that Paul had requested a special meeting with the *chargé d'affaires* and the agency heads, but it couldn't be scheduled before he left for the beach. That's a really unusual request, isn't it? What do you suppose it was about?"

"Huh, that's truly odd. I wonder if he told anyone anything about what he wanted."

Ruth said "Maybe he did, and that person took action to make sure he didn't tell anyone else."

"Oh, come on, Ruth! You are being melodramatic, don't you think? This isn't a paperback detective novel, with Miss Marple in the sittingroom with a sherry and a magnifying glass." Paul stood up and stretched, then sat down again and said "Well, it looks like Eleanor and Bernie may have split up. She's "going on vacation" without the kids or Bernie. I heard she was on the PanAm flight out of here today, en route to the US via Sydney."

"Mark Fairchild! You 'forgot' to tell me that? Could this whole thing be an investigation into the commissary funds? Quite a lot of money must pass through there in a month. Looks like she's getting out of Dodge just one jump ahead of the law!"

"Could be, I suppose. There must be contracts with suppliers and all that. Kickbacks, perhaps? But Eleanor would need someone to help her — the commissary operates independent of the embassy, except that the embassy arranges import licenses for supplies from outside Indonesia. Things like cigarettes and alcohol—the controls on import of those are pretty strict, so the embassy has to use its diplomatic privilege to get them in. There would need to be government purchase orders and accounting."

"Would she have to work with George Stewart?", Ruth asked "or is there someone else in the admin office that would deal with those things? Nini, George's pretty 'assistant', for example?"

"Someone else would do the work, but George is the Administrative Officer, so he has the ultimate responsibility for oversight, and he'd be the one to sign off on any purchase orders, etc., so he would have ..." Mark broke off as the doorbell began to bong continuously, and there was loud hammering on the front door. Simultaneously, the rain began pounding down again — well, thought Ruth, at least I know the doorbell works!

"Who can that be?" Mark said, as he got up to answer the door but it flew open before he could get there. Four Indonesian military policemen burst in, with guns drawn and pointed at Mark and Ruth.

Mark stood his ground. "WHAT THE HELL? GET OUT!" he shouted "I am an American diplomat and this is diplomatic territory. You are in violation of every goddamned treaty known to man. Put the guns away, and we can talk. What the hell do you want?"

The servants had heard the din and were in a frightened huddle at the kitchen door, while the deluge continued to roar, the roof began to leak again, and Zoe plodded through complaining softly about her wet feet, shaking each one in turn before proceeding. Looking over the pathetic scene, the officer in charge gave an order, and the squad put away their guns, looking a little disappointed, as if they had expected more drama and excitement. "Okay" yelled Mark "that's better. Now, what do you want?"

"We want the tree" said the officer "the tree in the pot."

"What?" said Mark "What are you talking about?"

Ruth though realized what he wanted—Eleanor's palm—and found her voice. "It's not here. Ñoña Jackson took it away the other day. Why do you want it?"

"Ñoña, it is evidence in a murder case. It is necessary that it be examined by us."

"Well, you can't," said Ruth. "It's not here. So, leave before we call the President and complain about your violation of diplomatic immunity."

The officer gave an order and, surprisingly, the group shuffled out, looking a little embarrassed as well as reluctant to brave the raging torrent of rain. When they had gone, Ruth said "Mark, you really took control! How did you know what to do? I am still shaking! And, is our house really US territory?"

Mark replied "I don't think so, but they don't know either. Worked though, didn't it? I'll call the embassy, get some security help here. And now, what is it with these damned palms—now they're evidence in a murder case?"

Chapter Ten

Jakarta, 1968

"Ruth, are you alright? Rob called me when he got to work this morning, to tell me what happened here last night! You must have been terrified! Did you get any sleep?" Gwen rushed in, talking before she was through the door.

Ruth, reclining on the sofa with Zoe on her lap, started to laugh, a bit wearily. "Yes, I'm fine, thanks! But what an evening. I must say, I saw a side of my husband that I hadn't known existed—he was amazing! But we're both tired this morning, and the house is a waterlogged mess. Please sit down, if you can find a dry seat." Zoe stood up and stretched, then jumped down, and Ruth continued "the embassy sent a couple of the marine guards here for the night, and the doctor came and gave me a sedative. Mark is at the office dealing with the fallout today — a formal note of protest to the Ministry of Foreign Affairs, demands for explanation, etc."

"Rumor has it that this has made large waves in Washington" Gwen said, "as it should! What exactly happened — Rob didn't have any details."

"You know how it was raining — Biblical downpours, noise, the roof leaking like it was made of straw, and four men in uniform pushing their way in with guns drawn, pointed at us — like a movie! We must have looked pretty pathetic, and at first, I thought it was a joke, but Mark immediately caught on and challenged them, told them to get out, and they backed down."

"I just can't imagine the scene! I would have been completely petrified!"

"Well, I was at first. And the rainstorm was pretty scary too — does it rain like that every day?"

Gwen laughed, "In the rainy season — most days, yes! And not to belittle things, but everyone's roof leaks. The women's association has a rainy season contest to see who has the most buckets in use on a daily basis."

Ruth went on talking nervously, "But when Mark yelled at them 'what do you want?' and they said 'the tree in the pot', I almost burst out laughing at the silliness. They wanted Eleanor's palm — said it is 'evidence in a murder case' — that stupid ugly plant."

She stood up. "Let's go and sit in the garden and leave Siti and Hindun to try to get the house straightened up. The garden must be a mess, but Zoe would like a sunbath anyway, and we can have coffee and talk."

They walked out together into the humid sun-splashed garden. Contrary to Ruth's expectations, the plants looked freshly washed, water droplets sparkling in the sunlight, new flowers unfolding from the hibiscus, with no trace of the wild weather of the night. The birds in the big cage fluttered and chattered happily, as Ruth checked that the chairs were dry enough to sit on. As they settled themselves, Zoe ambled out followed by Siti with a cushion for the cat's chair. "Nothing is too much trouble for Princess Zoe around here, you see!" said Ruth, as Zoe jumped onto the cushion, turning around three times before curling herself into a tidy loaf to prepare for her sunbath. "She thinks she fell into a tub of cream!"

"Ruth, Eleanor flew off 'on vacation' yesterday, did you hear? Imaginations are running wild, and the grapevine is humming!"

"Yes, Mark told me that last night. And," Ruth went on "whose was the body floating in the pool? I've heard everyone now, from the King of Siam to Ho Chi Minh." Zoe, hearing Ruth's voice raised, slitted one blue eye open but decided that nothing worth her attention was happening, put a paw over her eyes to block the sun, and went to sleep.

"Making my calls yesterday was interesting! Everyone wanted to talk about the body in the pool and Paul's disappearance, and I ended up taking a long time to get through because they all pressed me to stay; I couldn't tell them anything though, and Belinda would be scandalized at how long I stayed at some of the houses. She's probably angry that I kept her car so long. I hope no-one tells her I wasn't wearing stockings!"

"Well," began Gwen, "it looks as if someone gained after-hours entry to the pool area through one of the embassy houses that back up to it. They are all occupied by US embassy staff, and it's supposed to be only possible to get into the pool area by using a special code to open the back gate. So, they're talking to the residents of those houses now. Might take a while, since there are ten houses, and apparently most of the servants have the codes too, so that they can let the kids out to the pool. And really, it wouldn't be impossible to climb over the gates or the fence."

Ruth, frantically trying to get up to speed on what was going on, said "I haven't been to the pool yet, so I can't picture it. Do I know any of the people who live there?"

"Your new friend Helke Ramsey and her husband, but their kids are young teens so the servants wouldn't need the code for the gate, but she's a bit casual and might have left it around for anyone to find. Let's see ... Oh, Eleanor and her husband live there. They have two children, so the servants and/or the kids will have the code as well. I'm not sure ... I think Paul Faber might have lived in one of those houses too."

"Yes — Helke said he lived there and he wasn't happy because of all the after-hours parties. That reminds me..." Ruth interrupted herself "someone yesterday, I think it was at the AID director's house, said that she heard that Paul had been worried about something. He had asked for a meeting with the *chargé d'affaires* and the agency heads, but he disappeared a couple of days before the meeting was to take place."

"What?" Gwen blurted, surprised. "He was worried about something? No hints about what? It must have been something that concerned the post. If it had been a family or personal thing, he would have just asked for compassionate leave to go home, or talked it over with friends, but not requested a meeting with the top brass of the embassy."

The phone began to ring—almost the first time it had worked— causing Ruth to think that maybe she had chosen the right offering for the *telopon*; maybe now was the time to find out what the roof needed, so that they could retire the bucket brigade and sleep without wet feet from the leak above the bed. But first things first — answer the magical instrument!

Ruth gestured to Gwen to wait a moment and picked up the phone. A male American voice said "Is this Mrs. Fairchild?" Ruth, surprised, assented, and the caller went on: "This is George Stewart, in the admin office. We met the other day when you came by, and I wonder if you are free to come to the office now to help with a matter concerning your household?"

"My husband is in the embassy now. Could he help with this, since he's there?"

"Afraid not; he says you are the one to talk to. Could you come down, or could I come to your house for a few minutes?"

"If you could come here, that would be good. I'm here all morning."

"Thanks. I'll be there in a half hour." Ruth hung up, and turned to Gwen.

"That was George Stewart, he who said he didn't know who Suleiman had worked for! He has questions for me! I have some for him, but I need to think about strategy, don't you think? Let's try to hear him out without saying anything", and she and Gwen sat speculating until an embassy car pulled into the driveway and George Stewart got out and walked across the lawn to them. An attractive man, Ruth realized, with an air of authority -- the man who might be looked to as the leader in a group. "Hi, Gwen. Ruth — nice to see you again." They shook hands, and Ruth asked if he would prefer to meet inside, or would he like to stay in the garden. He chose the garden, Siti brought coffee, and they settled again. "Is it alright if Gwen stays?"

"Fine, no problem. In fact, it could be helpful." His voice was unusual, Ruth thought — deep but gentle, pleasantly warm and without a noticeable accent. "Gwen, Mark told me you were here with Ruth the other day when the incident with the knife happened?"

"Not right then. I was here earlier, and came back later in the day to help Ruth deal with the situation and translate for her."

George pulled out a tattered envelope and selected a couple of photographs; he passed one to Ruth and asked her "do you recognize either of these?" The first photo showed an Indonesian man, dressed in the typical work garb of white shirt and trousers, standing in front of a tall closed gate. The house behind was large, and appeared to be the kind of expansive residence inhabited by upper-level foreigners. Ruth began to say that he looked like Suleiman, her former cook, but decided not to say anything because she wasn't quite sure. And, she was beginning to wonder about the wisdom of volunteering any information till she had a better idea of what was going on.

She passed the photo to Gwen, who shook her head indicating that she didn't recognize him but asked "That's one of the old colonial houses in Menteng — any idea whose it is?"

"The house is the Soviet ambassador's residence" answered George curtly, clearly not wishing to say more.

The other photo was a close-up of a watch, showing the face and the reverse in detail. Gwen said "it's a Patek Phillipe, but not a new one... I can't read the inscription though — is that French? "

Ruth spoke up — "yes, it's French. 'Bonne Chance! Papa'. Means 'Good Luck! Dad'. It's an expensive French watch, but I have never seen it before that I know of. Should I recognize it?"

"Probably not" George said, "but it's worth checking. Thank you, ladies, for your help." He rose and drained his coffee cup, scritched Zoe behind the ear and started to leave. He stopped, turned around and said "Ruth, we think the man in the photo might be your former cook. Are you sure you don't recognize him? He — Suleiman— was found floating in the embassy swimming pool with this watch on his wrist and a knife in his back."

Chapter Eleven

Meeting with George Stewart

A few days after the armed invasion of their home, another call from George Stewart surprised Ruth and Mark; hinting that he might have some information of interest to them, he asked if they could meet him for a few minutes at a cafe in the nearby market complex. Reluctantly they agreed to meet him.

As they left their house on foot, the Call to Prayer was sounding from the local mosque, and people were walking hastily in that direction for afternoon prayer. The heat was declining as the sun sank lower in the sky and shadows lengthened with the approach of evening. As they walked, they listened to the chant of the muezzin from the tall minaret; Ruth said "I enjoy hearing it from the house. Do you know what the words mean?"

Mark answered "I don't know all of the words, but I know the beginning:

'God is Great! God is Great! God is Great! God is Great! I bear witness that there is no god except the One God.'

I think it repeats 'God is Great' again — I learned a little of it when I took that trip to Central Asia while we were in Moscow. And yes, I agree — I like hearing it during the day when we're at home. Interesting to live in a Muslim country, isn't it? Especially this one, with its under layers of Hindu and Buddhist faiths. So much to learn!"

Once again, Ruth was surprised by Mark. He still looks like what he was when we met — a farm boy, just arrived in DC from his mid-Western college, full of energy and amusing naivety, charming and funny. But he's more than that now—well, he always was, really —and people don't realize that there is a sophisticated mind at work behind the Gee Whiz facade. He didn't have to learn the words of the Call to Prayer, he did it because he is curious and likes to acquire knowledge for its own sake, to enrich his life.

It seems to help him feel in control of things too, and he does like to be in control of everything, including me. He doesn't yet get that I am an independent person, with my own needs and wants. I love him, I am happy with him, but sometimes I wish there were more ways for wives to achieve something in the foreign service. Giving lovely parties, dressing well, being charming to important people may help his career but it doesn't help me be fulfilled and satisfied. Some people call foreign service wives the "American geisha"! Well, a topic for another day, she thought.

Ahead of them was Blok M, their destination— a large building, walls stained with black mildew, with an outdoor market and arcades containing shops and restaurants. A lively scene, busy with vendors and shoppers enthusiastically bargaining for wares from all over southeast Asia— stalls overflowing with fruit and vegetables, meat and fish, noodles and spices, dishes and textiles, kettles and pots, beds and chairs and shoes and buckets and mops. "Stewart said he would meet us in Sarinah Cafe, in Arcade B. Let's see how this place is organized" said Mark, as they made their way through the customers and the flock of begging small boys — "Tuan, me watch car? One rupiah, only. Me no steal, no like others."

"Just as well our car isn't here yet." Ruth said, laughing at the bright-eyed enthusiasm of the children, none of whom appeared hungry although their clothes were shabby. "This looks like an after-school game! There's Sarinah, on the left up ahead. It's crowded. Hope we can find a table."

"There's Stewart in front, waving to us" Mark answered, waving back as he helped Ruth through the crowd to the cafe. The smoke in the room was thick and the floor sticky; the small tables surrounded by sagging rattan chairs were slightly grease-stained, and Ruth hoped that there were no biting cane bugs in the chairs. She found the mingled smells of mildew, *kretek* cigarettes, and dried fish almost sickening, and the lazily-revolving ceiling fans did nothing to improve the atmosphere. They settled at a table and ordered *kopi susu* — strong local coffee tamed and sweetened with condensed milk, while George Stewart rummaged through a folder he laid on the table.

Stewart, a tall man of solid build, had short neatly-trimmed light brown hair and a pleasant expression. His very light blue eyes, incongruous in his tanned and strongly modeled face, were sharp, leading Ruth to think that he could be a precise and careful man of definite opinions, not easily swayed. "Thanks for coming, Fairchilds" he said. "I wanted to talk to both of you, and I think it's best if we talk away from the office or your house."

"What are you implying?" Mark reacted quickly. "Is there some reason that we shouldn't talk in those places? What is going on here?"

"To be honest, I don't know if anything is going on, but at the moment there are so many unanswered questions that I am trying to limit the possibility of gossip or mischief if something is overheard." He turned to Ruth "Mark called me and told me that you had some questions, and some thoughts about your cook, Suleiman. What can I tell you?"

"Yes, I do have some questions, and I think I can also tell you something that might be important — do you have a photograph of the knife that was ... um ...?"

"In the body? Yes." Stewart rummaged through his file for a moment, and produced a large black and white photograph showing the handle of a knife. "It's bigger than it looks in the photo, the handle is around 7" long, while the blade is a bit longer — about 8 1/2"." It's quite sharp, and an efficient weapon, really."

Ruth looked at the photo for a moment, then handed it back to Stewart. "Yes, I believe that's the knife that my cook was stropping during the short time he was working at our house. It was unnerving."

"So, you are identifying it positively as belonging to Suleiman?"

"Yes. Now that I see it again, I am certain it's the same knife."

"Thank you. That is really helpful. An embassy staff member has identified the man who died as Suleiman, your former cook—he knew him when Suleiman was working as a driver for Paul Faber. Apparently, he drove for Paul for a while, and he and Paul seemed to get along very well."

Ruth, still not completely trusting Stewart, asked "Why did you say you didn't know much about him when I came to the office that day?"

"Yes, I can see why you are wondering about that. I'm sorry — I knew only what I told you about him when you asked about his references. He didn't appear on any of our current lists, and I am not sure how Paul found and hired him. I would like to know that too."

Mark broke in "Well, how did he get into our house then? Did you place the others there? And do you know about their references?"

"Yes, they're all either on our list or referred by their colleagues, but I just don't know how Suleiman was hired. For example, Muriarti has a long record of working for embassy families, and she brought Siti along a few years ago. Siti is her sister-in-law. I hired the whole crew other than Suleiman — are you happy with them?"

Ruth replied "they're great, and I have no worries about them. But I have some other questions."

"I 'll do my best to answer them. But first — Suleiman's death. He was not killed with the knife. We believe he was beaten to death elsewhere, brought to the pool area after death, then dumped into the pool and the knife stuck in his back, probably for dramatic effect."

Ruth and Mark were quiet as they considered this information. It seemed so improbable that someone they knew, who had been in their house as an employee so recently, should have been brutally murdered and his body dumped in a public place apparently as a message of some kind. The noisy bustle surrounding them in the cafe seemed to fade for Ruth, and she reached for Mark's hand to anchor her in this time and place. Why, she thought? Then realized that she had spoken aloud, as Stewart answered her "We don't know. We are trying to trace his movements, find out who knew him, what he was doing in the past ten days since you dismissed him. There are a couple of leads, not great but ..."

"Another question, Stewart" said Mark "we wonder who did the packing of Paul's stuff and the inventory of his effects? I've never had any experience of someone dying on post — and someone without a family with them makes it trickier, I guess. I have no idea how such a thing is handled, but there must be regulations for such an event. Where were his things sent? Did he have a family at home? Did he have a will? Who's in charge of this mess?"

Stewart, the careful man that Ruth had discerned, spoke thoughtfully and precisely, after a long pause. "Well, I guess I am. I was an attorney before I got into the foreign service—being an FSO is a lot more fun than practicing law, I find—and I think everything has been done according to the books. Yes, there is an inventory, done by Joe and Belinda Forrest and checked by me before everything was sent to his sister in Chicago, who is listed as his next-of-kin."

"And a will?", queried Ruth, unable to hold still another minute for Stewart to pause again. Yes, she thought, he certainly acts like a lawyer — looks at everything from eight sides, ties himself up in questions, ponders, ruminates, considers, objects, reflects. At last —

"This is totally confidential, and I am telling you because you have become involved involuntarily. Yes. There is a will—he sent it to his sister to hold for him and it has been opened since his disappearance. We don't know what it means. It has caused consternation in Washington, and is one of the reasons for the surprise inspection. You see, Paul had quite a large estate inherited from his parents, both lawyers in a large Chicago law firm. A family of almost irreproachable respectability—father of French descent--a little questionable in Chicago eyes but ..., mother from ultra-middle-class Evanston...Lake Shore Drive apartment, house in Winnetka, generations of solid financial means." Ruth snorted mentally. He means rich, dull and boring.

"In a will dated six months ago, Paul left everything to Nina Petrovna Smirnova. She is the wife of the current Soviet ambassador to Indonesia."

Chapter Twelve

Gamelan

"You knew about Paul's affair with her and you didn't tell me? How the hell did you know? And why didn't you ....?"

"Calm down and stop shouting at me, Mark! What I heard was a bit of gossip and I didn't want to make too much of it. I didn't think the source was reliable, and it seemed so improbable anyway."

Just home from their meeting with George Stewart, Ruth and Mark were trying to discuss his revelations quietly and rationally, although the daily deluge of rain and Mark's exasperation at being blindsided made it difficult. The roof still leaked after the repairs had been made but now in different places, presumably where the workmen had walked on the friable tiles. Perhaps it would be best to just mark where the worst ones are, put buckets there, and put up with it; it can't rain like this forever, thought Ruth.

"Who is this Solange woman? How did you meet her?" Mark was pursuing the topic doggedly, not ready to drop it yet.

"I told you — her husband's something at the French Embassy and I met her at lunch the other day. I told you about going to lunch with Gwen after we saw George Stewart about Suleiman. You brushed it off as frivolous female chatter, so I dropped it." Ruth felt she had scored a point here, and Mark took a minute to respond.

"Alright, maybe I did. I'm sorry. So, tell me again what she said?"

Ruth, still ruffled at having been shouted at, sighed a bit theatrically and began to relate Solange's story as told to her and Gwen on the ride home from lunch. Zoe arrived and jumped into Ruth's lap, turning her back on Mark as if to exclude him from the scene. As she stroked the purring cat, Ruth finished the recap and said "So. That's all I know. End of story. I thought it was pretty odd, maybe a sophisticated honey trap, but the will puts it all into a new light, doesn't it?"

"I am going to guess that this is what Paul wanted to talk to the embassy brass about" Mark said "but what was he planning to say?"

"I wish I knew!" breathed Ruth fervently. "We'd better get moving. The Ramseys will be here soon to pick us up for the dance performance tonight. I don't know what to wear."

A half hour later the rain had stopped, and Mark called "Let's go, Ruth! The Ramseys are here", as Helke and Howard Ramsey's car pulled into the driveway. "We'll have to discuss Stewart's revelations later. A lot to process, there. You look great — I like that dress!"

Is that an apology, wondered Ruth. Must be, but we still have to talk about that whole thing.

As they greeted the Ramseys and climbed into the car, Ruth noticed that it was cool inside. "Oh, how marvelous! Are all the cars here air-conditioned? I don't think our new one is, and hardly any are in Europe. Such a pleasure in this climate!"

"Seems like a necessity to me" Howard Ramsey said "although not every car has it yet. Certainly makes a difference in daily life here!"

Helke said "I should tell you what we are going to see tonight at the *Hotel des Indes*. It's a performance of traditional dance from Java and Bali — I hope it won't be too touristy, but it will be interesting anyway. Have you seen any of these dances, and heard gamelan music?"

Ruth responded "I've heard some recordings of gamelan, but I don't know much about it, and I haven't seen any of the dances. I am really excited to see it for the first time, and thanks for including us tonight! I'm glad it stopped raining early, so the performance can go on."

"Yes, the dance stage at the hotel is outdoors, but I'm sure an army of people are busy drying things so that it can take place. And here we are."

The driver turned into a tree-shaded drive lighted by flickering kerosene torches and pulled up at a *porte cochere* where servants waited to open doors and direct guests to tables in a covered gallery with open arches on three sides, surrounding a central stage. They settled at their assigned table, and Ruth looked around at her surroundings. The stage, open to the sky, was backed by a stone wall with two split columns flanking a narrow entrance. Torches burned to either side of the entrance, illuminating strange trees, twisting lichen-covered branches with few leaves, and frangipani with their stark silhouette.

On the stage in front of the wall was arranged the gamelan — the larger gongs at the rear, suspended from racks with dragons carved on top, then the smaller hanging gongs, and in front of those low red and gold racks on which were placed small round gongs or flat metal bars which would be struck by the hammers and mallets of floor-seated musicians. A large open space in front of the instruments was reserved for dancers.

As Ruth studied this exotic assemblage, the musicians appeared through the central gate and took their places at their instruments, beginning to tune and adjust the gongs. Helke whispered to her "They are wearing informal dress — simple shirts and batik *kain* (skirts), because this is a recital and not a temple or palace ritual, but I hope the dancers are in full traditional dress —it's incredibly lovely."

It was hot -- will I ever get used to this blanketing humidity, wondered Ruth? Many women in the audience and some men too were using pretty folding fans, gilded bamboo ribs with dramatic batik coverings. Ruth thought of butterflies fluttering in the air and was reminded of the white-gloved hands of American tourists in the stuffy darkness of the Bolshoi in Moscow as they applauded the skill of the dancers.

The audience was settling down now, waiters had served drinks and snacks, and most tables were filled except for several in the center front, to which hotel functionaries were ushering a large group. The lights went down except for the torches on the stage, and the gamelan began to sound its rippling music. Suddenly a small figure appeared from the side—a golden apparition, long fingers tipped in gold, trembling flowers on the head glinting and flashing reflections from the torchlights. Then another from the other side, each like a gilded dragonfly. They danced together but alone, passing and repassing, sometimes mirroring the other's movements face-to-face, aware of one another but never touching and connected only by gesture and dramatic eye movements, their bodies tightly bound breast to thigh in stiff gold sashes, fingers elongated with golden fingernails, feet bare, stylized makeup on childish faces, heads crowned with shimmering wreaths of quivering golden flowers.

"They're *legong*" Helke murmured "very young girls, probably no more than 9 years old. The tradition's dying out now, tourist performances are given by teenage and older girls; this is truly old Bali."

It was pure enchantment to Ruth, beginning to end. When the last dancer had left the stage and the musicians laid down their hammers and mallets, the lights came up in the audience and she felt she had been in a dream. "Thank you so much, Helke, for showing this to me. I had no idea it would affect me so strongly."

"Perhaps you would like to come with me again — it takes a while to begin to see the subtleties of the different forms. It fascinates me, and I go to as many performances as I can!"

They began to gather their belongings, preparing to leave. Ruth noticed that the group of latecomers were doing the same thing and she saw Nina Petrovna among them, talking to another woman. Of course, this would interest her — she's a dancer, and I wonder if she is incorporating some of this into her own work. I hope she hasn't given up dance completely. Suddenly, Helke noticed her also, and said "Oh, there's Paul's friend. I don't know who she is, but she's striking, isn't she? "

"You have seen her with Paul?" squeaked Ruth, astonished.

"Yes — I used to see her by herself at dance performances, but one evening she was seated next to Paul. I don't know whether that's when they met, but after that … well, you know we live next-door to Paul's old house, and I used to see the two of them in the garden there sometimes—our house overlooks it." She paused for a moment to reflect "She is so beautiful, and I always wondered who she is but never had the nerve to ask him — and sometimes I would see her coming or going in his car, with Suleiman driving."

"Helke, she's Nina Petrovna Smirnova, the wife of the Soviet ambassador, and a former ballet dancer. And Paul left his estate to her in his will."

"Oh my … I knew he made a will last year — he came over one evening and asked Howard and me to witness his signature, but we didn't know what was in it. Well!" Helke chuckled, "At least Paul had some lovely times in that garden!"

"Have you told anyone else about this?"

"No. But ... I think there was someone else watching the garden too. I found a place where the plants were crushed down to make a space to look through. It seemed sinister to me and I thought about telling Paul, but Howard said to leave things alone and not get involved so I kept quiet."

Chapter Thirteen

Lunch at the Residence

So, thought Ruth as she rode in the embassy car on the way to lunch with Mrs. Rowlandson, wife of the current Ambassador Extraordinary and Plenipotentiary of the United States of America to the Republic of Indonesia, is my hat on straight? Are my gloves clean? And will she notice that I am not wearing stockings, per Belinda's edict?

The morning phone call from the ambassador's aide had given her little information, except that Mrs. Rowlandson had arrived back unexpectedly and would like to meet the spouses of newly assigned staff. Does this mean that Ambassador Rowlandson has returned also? It's a long time since he was here! Maybe this is their farewell appearance. Will I know anyone? I wish I had been able to talk to Mark or Gwen before I had to leave the house, but the *hantu telepon* wouldn't allow me to make any calls. Well, good luck to me, I'm on my own, she thought as the car turned into a drive leading through a thick tangled hedge of bougainvillea behind which was concealed a large house in the Dutch colonial style. Papaya trees like upended dish mops reared heads above the thorny colorful bougainvillea, velvet-green lawns interrupted by weedless flower beds surrounded the house, and she could glimpse swimming pool blue behind another smaller hedge of brilliant yellow hibiscus.

The white painted house, with its tile roofs, dark green shutters, and welcoming wide verandahs was beautiful, although to Ruth its size presented it as a place for the rich and powerful, the dominant members of its society, and made it perhaps unwelcoming to people of lesser importance.

The car swished gently up to the verandah which shaded the entrance to the house. Several women were standing at the door, chatting to a petite woman with alarming red hair. As Ruth alighted from the car, they moved on into the house and the redhead turned to greet her "Why, you must be Ruth Fairchild! I have been looking forward to meeting you ever since I learned you were here! My friend Vangie in Paris told me about you and here you are! Welcome, and come on in!"

Vangie in Paris? thought Ruth. Can she mean Evangeline Baxter, the wife of the US Ambassador to France? I met her once, in the receiving line at a big reception. These ladies have an intelligence network that puts the KGB to shame—ambassadorial aides cross-referencing annotated guest lists Paris-Jakarta, 3x5 card files indexed "Dinner", "Reception", "Lunch", even "Tea", with notes of menus served to invitees on such and such a date, at which kind of event, other card files recording number of guests, dress worn by Mrs. Ambassador, any special happenings (i.e., caterer dropped the bowl of shrimp, performing seals got loose, guest-of-honor got drunk, pinched the hostess, and so on) So, Vangie told her about me — I wonder what she said?

Ruth's musings on foreign service entertaining were interrupted by Mrs. Rowlandson's suggestion that she and Ruth proceed through the house to the verandah. There they found six others seated comfortably in wide rattan chairs with soft cushions, chatting pleasantly while servants served drinks and passed hors d'oeuvres. Among the guests was Eleanor, prim in her chair and still dressed for air travel. Feet neatly together in pretty shoes, her dress conservatively covering her knees, her bag placed tidily on the floor at her feet and wearing a winsome little hat — she was the very picture of a junior diplomat's wife, anxious to find favor with the spouse of the ambassador.

What on earth—where did she come from? I thought she had run away- thought Ruth as she acknowledged Mrs. Rowlandson's introductions of the others in the group, of whom she had met only Gwen. And, of course, Eleanor. "Ruth and I are already friends" said Gwen with a smile "Come and sit next to me, Ruth. This chair's not taken." Smiling charmingly, she turned to Eleanor and asked "So — how was your vacation? Did you go home to California?"

A subdued reply from Eleanor "No, there wasn't time. I was in Sydney."

Mrs. Rowlandson said "Sydney is my favorite city! I always arrange to travel that way so that I can shop and get my hair done. What did you do while you were there?"

"Mostly work. I had some business appointments, some new commissary suppliers to interview, things like that."

"When did you get back?" asked one of the other guests.

"This morning, on the PanAm flight. I haven't been home yet — came directly here from the airport when I received the lunch invitation."

Just then, a servant entered and whispered something to Mrs. Rowlandson, who said "Eleanor, there is an embassy car at the door to pick you up and take you to the embassy. I'm told that you must go directly there, without stopping anywhere. I'll see you to the door."

Eleanor stood up, eyes welling with tears "No, no, please! I came back to see my kids and I haven't had a chance to see them yet. Please let me go home." She was trembling, crying in earnest now, tears running down her cheeks as she pleaded to be allowed to go home. All the blithe assurance that Ruth had seen in her when she came to take the palm was gone, replaced by an apparently overwhelming fear.

Mrs. Rowlandson, looking somewhat shaken herself, took her arm and said "Come, Eleanor. I'll walk with you." To the other ladies in the group, she said "Is there anyone who could accompany Eleanor in the car to the embassy?" Ruth and Gwen both indicated that they could do so, and the ambassador's wife said "That's good! Let's get moving now" and, taking Eleanor's arm, preceded them out of the verandah, saying as she left "Well, so much for my little lunch party! We will have to try again another day." Ruth reflected — well, what will go on the "Lunch" card for today? "Amusing diversion--arrest of embassy spouse, wore my pink dress. Hair needs color."?

The drive to the embassy was brief, but Eleanor broke her silence, saying "It's all just awful! Florin dumped me in Sydney, took my money and my air tickets and left me there. I had to call Bernie to get me back here. And now I guess the inspectors want to talk to me about things! I wish I was dead." When they reached the embassy, a marine guard was waiting for her at the main door and took her arm to lead her into the building. The tears began again as she left the car.

Gwen's car and driver were waiting for them—efficient staff work by Mrs. R's secretary, Ruth guessed—and they were free to do whatever they pleased. "Street food, Ruth?" asked Gwen. "There's a good place nearby, and we won't meet anyone we know there. Let's go talk!"

They settled on stools at a tiny table under an umbrella in the street where vendors sold their food from carts and folding tables, and the scent of grilling meats and spicy sambals wafted around them. Gwen brought Ruth her order of chicken satay on a green banana leaf, with a questioning tilt of the head as she offered sauce — "Yes, please — I love the peanut sauce!"

"Any ideas on the Eleanor situation?" Gwen asked, sitting down with her banana leaf plate on which were sliced wilted cucumber, and two little *martabak* pastries filled with spicy meat. "Shouldn't eat the cucumber from street vendors, I know, but it's delicious."

"No ideas about Eleanor" replied Ruth "her question — 'why did I come back' was pretty interesting, implying that she had an alternative. Without money or tickets what was she going to do?"

"Why is she so scared? I mean — the woman was trembling all over in the car. I suppose she can't expect much more than minimal help from her husband, after running off with another man, but Bernie doesn't seem like someone who could be violent."

Ruth thought for a moment "well, at least he got her out of a bad situation in Sydney. But — did you notice that the servant's message to Mrs. Rowlandson was very short. I think she knew in advance that the car was coming to get Eleanor, and it was planned carefully to avoid a big scene. When were you invited?"

"This morning. As it was, the scene was pretty upsetting anyway! Mrs. R. looked upset, even her hair seemed to pale. Well, Ruth — remember when I told you there were strange happenings here? Was I right? What's your guess — kickbacks from commissary suppliers, fiddling the books for money to gamble in the Chinese gambling halls?"

Ruth burst out "I've been thinking about that. Remember the potted palm? I think she came to get it because there was something hidden in there that would establish a connection between her and Suleiman. When I fired him, it made it impossible for him to get back into the house to get it, so she had to come herself. Could it have been kickback money?"

"Drug money! She planted Suleiman and the palm in your house, he was her bagman, collecting money from the dealers in the area! That makes sense! Could that be why he was killed?" Gwen stopped and Ruth cut in:

"Makes me wonder — but why, and what does Eleanor have to do with it?"

Chapter Fourteen

George Stewart Makes a Move

"Have a good trip, Mark! Watch out for tigers!" Ruth waved as the embassy car taking Mark to the airport pulled out of the drive. Sumatra, she thought. I wonder if those stories about tigers still around over there are true.

The morning sun filtered into the living room, and she decided to sit down with another cup of coffee and read the two-week old copy of Time magazine that Mark had brought home last night. Nothing could be older than yesterday's newspaper, unless it was a two-week old news magazine, but at the least it brought something more than the bare outlines in the embassy's daily newsletter, or the uneasy English of the Jakarta Times. Vietnam, the assassinations of Martin Luther King and Robert Kennedy, riots at the Democratic Convention — so much unrest at home!

We live in a fragile bubble here, she thought, seemingly separated in time and space from the clamorous events of the outside world. We're still in the foreign service of the 30s —women are always "spouses" and spouses always women, no married woman can be a foreign service officer, and the wives are there to charm and entertain, to support their husbands, and to behave discreetly. A married officer is an advantage to the Department — "two for the price of one" has been said often. This life is not what I expected when Mark joined the foreign service. Can I live with this role forever? Is it enough for me to be an

American geisha, smiling and hospitable but without independent agency?

She heard a car entering the driveway, then the sound of another behind it. Car doors opened and closed, men's voices gave instructions, and the doorbell rang unexpectedly. Siti ran from the kitchen and admitted George Stewart. "George! I wasn't expecting you. Mark's away for a few days. Is there something I can do for you?"

"Hi, Ruth! I have a surprise for you — your car arrived yesterday, and we just finished unpacking it and getting it ready for you. It's in the drive, and I wanted to introduce your new driver also. Come on out." He took her arm and led her out to the driveway.

The car, an Australian Holden, had right hand drive and two doors. Not luxurious, but practical for local conditions. "Ruth, this is Muhammad. He was engaged for you a couple of weeks ago, to start work when your personal car arrived. Muhammad, this is Nõña Fairchild" Muhammad, a man of about 25, tall for an Indonesian, greeted her in accented English, saying "I hope I will be satisfactory, Nõña. I have been driving for an Australian family for several years; they have recently left."

Ruth extended her hand and they shook hands. "I am very glad to meet you, Muhammad. Please go into the house and meet everyone. I'm sure Muriarti will have coffee and something for you to eat." She turned to George and asked if he would care for coffee.

As they settled in the living room, he said "I hear Mark's gone to Sumatra this week — that's an interesting trip. How are you going to fill your time while he's gone?"

Slightly surprised by the question—why did George Stewart care how she spent her time—Ruth replied "Oh, I need to do some housekeeping things, go to the commissary, stock the *godown* with extra food, more buckets, etc. But I was hoping you could tell me more about Eleanor. What happened when she talked to the inspectors?"

"Turns out that Eleanor has been taking kickbacks from merchants and suppliers, here and in Australia. She was making quite a lot of money at it, and much of it appears to have gone to Florin Radu, the man who stranded her in Sydney. She was planning to return to the States with him. He had other ideas, I guess. He's gone, and we don't know where he went. The whole thing's pretty tough on Bernie and the kids."

"Kickbacks — well, I'm not surprised! Gwen and I had guessed something of the kind. Sorry about her family, but pretty stupid of her. What about the potted palms?"

"They were part of it — sold to the embassy for an artificially high price, percentage to Eleanor. Oh — she was also gambling and losing big with the high rollers down in the Chinese gambling parlors. Gambling is illegal here, but a lot goes on anyway and the authorities mostly look the other way."

"No, I really mean the potted palm she took from this house." Ruth said, "The day she came here, I think she came just to pick it up. That visit was so strange, and then during the armed invasion, they wanted to know where it was — the 'tree in the pot'. Said it was 'evidence in a murder case'!"

"Ruth" George said slowly "We aren't sure yet. Something was hidden in that pot, but we can't quite get the confirmation we need. I won't say any more, but you will be the first to know what happens. For now, Eleanor is under informal house arrest, and she'll be leaving for the US as soon as possible. The Indonesian government doesn't want to prosecute for the kickbacks—that's pretty much business as usual here—so unless something more serious about the pot turns up, she'll be off the legal hook. She wasn't taking commissary money, so there's nothing the embassy can do."

He picked up the magazine Ruth had been reading, and began to leaf through it. She interpreted this as a signal that he had finished his business and that no more information would be forthcoming right now. As he handled the magazine, she noticed his hands — broad, long fingered, capable, carefully manicured and maintained. Nice hands, a more attractive man than I thought at first. Those very light blue eyes are startling in his tanned face. I wonder what his story is.

"Well," he said, putting down the magazine "almost time for lunch. Would you be interested in joining me? Somewhere better than Cafe Sarinah, this time? There's a place I know down at the port where we could talk over a glass of wine. I'd like to know more about you." Smiling, he reached out and took her hand.

Oh, dear. Panicky, she thought — Mark's gone, he's decided it's a good time for a move. I really wasn't expecting this! I don't want to antagonize him—we might need him sometime. Here's a pretty mess ... how do I handle it?

"Anybody home? Ruth?" called a voice from the front door, and Helke Ramsey walked in, smiling and fresh, her short dark hair curling around her lively face, and carrying a baguette and a little white grocery bag. "Brought some good bread and spicy shrimp for lunch!" Then, as she saw George and Ruth and caught George's quick dropping of Ruth's hand, "Oh, sorry! Didn't mean to interrupt!"

"Helke! Lovely to see you! George just brought our new car — did you see it outside?"

"Yes" said George, getting to his feet "And I was about to leave. Glad the car's here, Ruth!" He took her hand and squeezed it gently, gave her a long intense look, and walked out the door. The embassy car backed out and he was gone.

Ruth's panic subsided with his departure and she managed a polite welcome for Helke "Thank you for bringing lunch, Helke — what a good idea! Let's eat under the mango tree; I'll show you my new orchids while you're here."

"Howard said Mark's gone to Sumatra on an oil company trip. We did that last year, and I saw a tiger! He was lying on the grass under a tree, looking like a big housecat!"

"Wow! But speaking of tigers, tell me about George Stewart. He just made a pass at me."

"Oh, that man! Are you alright?"

"Oh, I'm fine, just a bit surprised! Not a common occurrence in my life!"

"Yes, I wondered when I saw him here! Well — he's married but he's a bit of a swinger, wife's not here — stayed in the States. He had an Indonesian girlfriend until recently but she went back to Cirebon, so he's on the loose again. The girl was thinking marriage, I guess, but George's not going to get out of his comfy convenient marriage to start again with someone new. Too much trouble. Do you think he's attractive?"

"Yes, but no. He came on very strong just now, and I don't think things would stop at lunch together. Too used to having his own way, maybe. Well, let's get Muriarti to put lunch out, and we can look at my new plants."

When Helke left, Ruth felt that she had made another friend, someone whose interests complemented her own, although I don't think she likes Gwen much. Good too that she arrived when she did, and George had been deflected. Somehow though I don't think he's put off for good. His sexual interest is very strong, I could feel it. My marriage is sound, she thought, I wouldn't want to damage it or do anything to hurt Mark. Proceed with caution in any contact with George Stewart, Ruth. But a little flare of interest lurked in her mind — he is a handsome man. What if ...

Chapter Fifteen

A Trip to the Country

The morning air was still. No breeze rattled the leaves on the banana tree as neighbor Mrs. Kang's roaming chickens scratched the dirt beneath it, clucking softly in their search for delicacies. In the kitchen, Muriarti supervised the huge pot set to boil the drinking water — ten minutes at the rolling boil needed for sanitation — as Ruth extracted two bottles filled with clean water from the kerosene refrigerator and put them in a basket with a handful of shrimp chips and some small sweet bananas, to share with Muhammad. He was in the driveway polishing the car, and seemed delighted at the prospect of a trip to the countryside, promising Ruth that he knew the very best nurseries, and that there was *banyak bensin,* plenty of gas, in the car.

I'm taking a trip, thought Ruth. All on my own today — no Mark, no friends. First time I have been out of the city since we arrived a month ago. Muhammad will be my guide, and I will begin to furnish the garden. And perhaps also begin to sort out my feelings about my life here and in the foreign service, and maybe remember Leonie with some happiness.

Muhammad driving sedately, they proceeded through quiet suburban streets past large houses with red tile roofs set in spacious gardens, encircled with stucco walls and tall metal gates. Some of the houses were hardly visible, defended by hedges of thorny bougainvillea or tousled mango and avocado trees with glossy dark green foliage, branches arranged perfectly for a child to climb and sit reading or dreaming, hidden from adult eyes. Between the fences and the street were deep drains with sloping sides built of large flat gray stones, holding pools of stagnant water filled with thready algae—monsoon drains, necessary to collect the water from the heavy rains of the wet season.

The car turned onto a larger road with more traffic, and sped up. Countryside now, rice *padis* bounded by grassy dikes supporting small flocks of geese, lumbering *karabao* — water buffalo —under the dubious control of small boys who lounged on the broad muddy backs waving thin reed switches, and ahead in the far distance, the outlines of mountains. A village appeared — white painted palm mat houses, vegetable gardens, mango trees spangled with fruit, pink-flowering frangipani trees spreading fragrance in the morning sun and then a small cemetery on the outskirts.

Past the cemetery, Muhammad slowed the car to avoid killing some of a flock of scrawny chickens which were picking at loose rice grains in the road; they scattered, squawking and protesting as the car turned onto a narrow path leading away from the main road. Very athletic chickens in Java, thought Ruth, as the car bumped gently over the rutted surface, no wonder their meat is so tough.

The car entered a small courtyard surfaced with rough gravel, and Muhammad pulled up beside a fat shiny black car, the only other one in evidence. A small house stood at one side of the space, its walls hung with lattice bearing numerous brilliantly colored orchids on slabs of bark or slatted wood baskets, and vines rambling over the walls and roof. "This is the best nursery here, people say", Muhammad offered, as Ruth stood staring at the exotic vegetation on display. "I will wait in the car, Nõña. When you are ready to buy, call me and I will help."

In a shade house, an enormous vine sprawled on an overhead trellis, branches thick as a man's wrist coiled around iron posts supporting it. Its long trusses of blood-red flowers dangled menacingly at Ruth's eye level, implying by their size and color that they were accustomed to red meat in their diet. Thinking she was alone, Ruth was startled when a woman's voice sounded from somewhere nearby "That is the most dangerous plant I have ever seen, I think! Would you plant it in your garden?"

Ruth replied to the as yet invisible speaker "Absolutely not! It looks as if it could easily consume you while you slept, doesn't it?", as a woman emerged from the tangle, and Ruth recognized her. Nina Petrovna Smirnova, wife of the Soviet ambassador and Paul Faber's lover! Ruth made a quick daring decision to introduce herself. "I'm Ruth Fairchild. I saw you at the gamelan and dance performance at *Hotel des Indes* a couple of weeks ago, and a friend told me your name. I am delighted to meet you!"

"I'm Nina Smirnova. You are a dance person?" Then, apparently as an afterthought, she asked "Did you say Fairchild? Did your husband replace Paul Faber as Economic Counselor in the US Embassy?"

"Yes. We arrived only a few weeks ago, and we are still getting settled. I don't really know about Indonesian dance, but I am anxious to learn about it. I imagine that you know a lot about it, with your training and background. My sister Leonie was a ballet dancer. She died last winter."

"Aaaah, you know about me, I see. I am sorry about your sister. Was she a good dancer?"

"I thought so. She was the principal dancer in a small troupe in Illinois -- nothing as glamorous as your career!"

"Glamor, glamor is nothing -- the love of ballet is the most important thing! Yes, Javanese and Balinese dance fascinate me. But I also love gardens, and want to replant the gardens at the residence to make them looser and more romantic, in the English style. At present, they are very Soviet, disciplined, stiff, and regulated, not romantic at all, and I would like to change that, so that's why I am haunting the nurseries around here."

"I have an empty garden, and I am trying to fill it with the beautiful things I see here—not that vine, though! You seem knowledgeable — perhaps you can help me learn?"

"That would be fun! And it would help my English too. Let's start now to choose something for your doorway. Plants at the door should be scented, don't you think?" They walked along together, the quicksilver dark Russian with the carriage of a princess, her fine-boned face, large eyes and graceful gestures combining in some intangible way to create extraordinary beauty. Beauty not only physical but with a clarity of intelligence and spirit; Ruth began to understand why audiences had found her so compelling a dancer, a sensitive interpreter of music, and to wish that she could have seen her in her previous milieu. She would have been a heartbreaking Juliet, she thought.

As they rounded a corner formed by a large flowering bush, Ruth saw a man walking toward them. Dark and heavyset, with a bad haircut and wearing an ill-fitting black suit, he was scowling as he peered around in the bushes in the dim light of the shade house; Ruth suddenly realized that Nina Petrovna was no longer at her side, and that she was alone and nervous. Passing the man and emerging into the sunlight of the parking place, she hoped to see Nina but it was empty except for the two cars. Muhammad appeared from her car, and she asked him to walk with her while she chose some orchids. He bargained for her purchases, and they returned to the car and drove away, seeing neither Nina Petrovna nor the man in the black suit again.

When they reached the village, Muhammad turned into a small road which ran behind the cemetery out of sight of the main road, saying "I must stop here for a minute." He pulled the car onto the verge and turned to her, handing her a tightly folded note and saying "the other lady gave this to me and said not to let anyone see me give it to you. I asked the nurseryman if he knows her and he said she comes there often, usually alone except for her driver."

Ruth, taking the note from him, said "Does he know her name?"

"I don't think so. He said she sometimes speaks a little Indonesian, and he has heard her speaking a foreign language to the driver. The driver is rude and never speaks to anyone but her. She used to have a different car and an Indonesian driver who was nicer."

"Thanks, Muhammad. Let's go on and I will read the note on the way home." Dying of curiosity now, Ruth unfolded the creased note, to read: "I am watched. I need to see you again. There is a trusted friend at this number. Leave a message and I will call when I can. Nina" with a Jakarta telephone number below.

The ride home seemed very short; she would arrive in time for lunch and escape the worst heat of the day. Ruth was preoccupied with thoughts of the events of the morning, and speculation about what would happen next. She was anxious to discuss it with Mark, who was due to return from his jaunt to Sumatra that evening. As they pulled into her driveway, she recognized the embassy car already there as the one George Stewart used, and found George himself sitting in the living room waiting for her.

"Ruth, I promised you would be the first to know if there was more information about Eleanor, but I insist that you let me take you to lunch so that I can tell you over a glass of wine what we have learned." Seeing her hesitation, he added "Come on, Ruth, it's only lunch."

Well, she thought. That's true. It's only lunch. How much trouble can I get into at lunch?

Chapter Sixteen

A Fishy Story

As Ruth left the house to join George in the embassy car, she heard him dismissing his driver, saying that he, George, would drive and telling him to wait at the Fairchilds' house for his return from lunch.

A little disconcerted by the fact that she would be alone with George for several hours, Ruth hesitated, but decided that changing her mind now would make it seem like a bigger and more significant event than just lunch. The driver helped her into the car, and they set off. "Have you been to Sunda Kelapa, Ruth?" George asked, as they turned onto a busy road. "It's the old port, also called Pasar Ikan — means Fish Market—and it's interesting. It's the best place to buy fish, and the shrimp are wonderful."

"I've hardly been out of Kebajoran Baru" replied Ruth. "This morning Muhammad took me to a plant nursery somewhere or other, to the east, I think. I could see mountains in the far distance."

"We're going northwest right now, heading for the Java Sea. The main port, Tanjung Priok, is very old, and was pretty well destroyed in WWII, but although Sunda Kelapa is actually older, it didn't have facilities for large ships so it escaped most of the destruction. It's not far from Jakarta — about 15 kms, and there isn't much traffic usually."

George talked for awhile about the history of Jakarta, using the old name, Batavia. "Did you know that Captain

Cook stopped here in 1770, on his way back to England from his circumnavigation of the globe? He lost a lot of men to fever here— very unhealthy place then, still is! Boil that water well!"

Ruth, listening to him, felt that he was a thoughtful and intelligent man and a pleasant companion, and as the conversation stayed general, she began to relax a little. It's only lunch, she told herself again, nothing to be ashamed of. They entered the town and pulled up near a wharf where there were a number of wooden ships tied up. The ships were painted bright blue, and had long high prows which extended gracefully over the edge of the wharf. The paint on some had faded to softer blue, and there were stylized eyes painted on their prows. "To see where they are going, of course. They are Buginese *pinisi* from Macassar, the merchant vessels of the archipelago. They carry everything from sugar to cattle to travelers" said George, as they left the car and began to walk toward a small group of buildings which housed a market.

Pasar ikan! Fish! Big fish, little fish, striped, dappled, red, shiny, silver, fish, octopuses, shrimp small to huge, torpedo tuna, fish unfamiliar and unnamable to Ruth. In a corner was a stall where a woman was selling intricate undamaged shells which had been caught in the fishermen's nets; Ruth thought that she would make a little collection of them and said "I hope there will be time after lunch to buy some; they would make a pretty display."

They climbed an outdoor staircase to a small open-air restaurant overlooking the wharf and the market, and sat down. Menus were brought, and George recommended a shrimp curry, saying lightly that some people consider shrimp a mild, magical aphrodisiac. Ruth said "No interest in aphrodisiacs, magical or otherwise, and just waiting for what you promised if I had lunch with you."

"You're a hard woman, Ruth! You look so soft and refined, with your blonde hair and blue eyes—that wholesome American girl innocence! It's quite beguiling, really -- makes a man want to investigate -- is it really innocence?"

"Makes me sound like a milkmaid! I'm not flattered."

"Alright, I meant it as a compliment, but I withdraw it. I will now pay my debt. Suleiman was apparently supplying Eleanor with drugs, which are highly illegal in Indonesia, death penalty stuff— execution by firing squad."

"Drugs! Death penalty! That's terrifying. Are you telling me that Eleanor was taking drugs?"

"No, we don't think so. We — the inspectors and investigating staff — know she was selling them to embassy personnel though. A lot of people at the post have come from Vietnam and casual drug use is epidemic there now because of the war. Suleiman was her supplier, and we don't yet know anything about his sources."

"But why were they in the potted palm?"

"Because you and Gwen fired Suleiman before he could get them to her. He must have received a delivery and decided that the bottom of the pot would be a safe place to hide them for a while. His room in your house had no lock and wouldn't have been safe, and then you took action and he couldn't get back into the house for them. He let Eleanor know what had happened, and she had to work out how to get them from there. Pretty creative thinking, don't you agree?"

"Drug dealing! That explains why she was so panic-stricken at the residence the other day! What is going to happen to her and how did you figure out that there were drugs in there? And why was he mad at my sweet Zoe?"

"Oh, Zoe — she apparently began to dig in the dirt in the pot, and he was scared she would somehow expose the package." He went on "Eleanor confessed. She thought the US government could save her. The embassy will have to turn her over to the Indonesian government for trial. It's not going to end well, but there isn't anything much we can do. Diplomatic immunity can't save her from this. We'll try, but we can only do so much."

"Oh, how dreadful! And Suleiman? Who killed him? And how did he get employed in my house?"

"Looks like Eleanor smuggled him onto the list somehow. We are still working on that. He has turned out to be an all-round bad guy, lots of shady connections, involved with crimes all over Jakarta — burglary, robbery, drugs — anything he could do to earn a dishonest living. Possibly he didn't pay his dealer and got killed for it."

Ruth wondered whether he knew that Suleiman had worked for Paul Faber, but decided to keep quiet about that for the moment, feeling that to mention it might draw more attention to Nina Smirnova's connection with Paul. "Well, you have answered a lot of questions, but left me with a lot more. I know Mark will want to talk to you too."

"Of course, no problem. And now, let's enjoy a glass of wine and lunch. Tell me about yourself."

"Pretty much what you see — married, coping with life in the foreign service, trying to stay afloat in a new, challenging place."

"I don't mean to seem rude, but you seem unhappy, Ruth. Are you bored? Do you like your life? You talk about "coping", "trying", "challenging" but you don't mention much happiness there. What would give you joy? Make you want to be in the moment of life? Do you know, or aren't you facing things yet?"

"I find this conversation impudent and inappropriate. I would like you to take me home now."

George laughed. "Don't be so prim, Ruth! Of course, I'm impudent and inappropriate—what did you expect? I'm supposed to be a wolf and a swinger, a seducer of maidens, charming but thoroughly dangerous. You must have heard that from the other women! But nonetheless you accepted my invitation to lunch and came. Why don't you just relax and enjoy the danger, like a lot of women do?"

"You seem proud of your bad reputation, and determined to practice on me."

With a sly smile, he said "True, but I know when I am not likely to get anywhere. Don't be too alarmed, but it could be fun to just flirt a little. Do you know how to do that? Most pretty women do, and it's amusing and harmless."

Despite her misgivings, Ruth couldn't help being amused, and rather surprised by George's charm. To be honest with herself, she wasn't happy, not really. Not bored, but my life seems futile. How could George have sensed that though? Mark is so busy at work, so engrossed in what he is doing, and there doesn't seem to be much room for me in his life any more. I have to build something for myself, and the standard embassy wife do-gooding is not it. I suppose for the moment, a little flirting couldn't hurt, as long as it's understood by both parties that it can't go any further.

"I don't think I know how to flirt!"

"You're doing it just fine right now, Ruth!" He reached out and brushed her hair away from her face, then took her hand on the table in both his hands. They were warm and dry. No sweaty palms or flabby hold, but a firm grasp, protective and enfolding. How pleasant, she thought, to feel protected, cared for, and valued for herself, but then, frightened by the feeling, she attempted to take her hand away. He grasped it more firmly and said softly "I could help you, Ruth. I could help you to settle here, to find satisfaction and pleasure, if you would just trust me. We could begin right here, this afternoon!"

Suddenly she realized that she was the bird, he the hypnotizing snake. "Trust me" sang the serpent, as the bird listened to its song and fell under its spell, only to wake up too late and be eaten. "George, take me home. Right now. This has gone quite far enough, and I am not interested in flirting with you!"

"Yes, ma'am! Straight home. But I'll be waiting, and we'll see what happens. You might be surprised by the world if you venture outside that protective shell you live in. Those shells you saw in the market are beautiful, but they don't let the creatures living inside grow. To do that, they have to abandon that temporary protection and move on."

"Yes" snapped Ruth "but without that protective carapace, they are completely vulnerable to predators. Home now."

Chapter Seventeen

Ruth Rebels

"Mark, it was just lunch!"

When Ruth came back from Sunda Kelapa, Mark had already arrived home from his trip to Sumatra, and saw George Stewart drive up with her in the front seat of the car.

"Ruth, George Stewart is a notorious womanizer! What is the matter with you, to expose yourself — and me, too — to vicious gossip? This will be all over the grapevine by tonight."

"Why are you so angry about this? A perfectly routine meal, out in the open in a restaurant with lots of other people around...how can people make gossip about that?" Is that all he cares about, thought Ruth, what people might think?

"Well, a couple of things. First, it was at the very least indiscreet, maybe stupid, to meet George Stewart alone, given his reputation. But more important — didn't you know that Sunda Kelapa is the local redlight district? And that the hotel there is generally the place for assignations among people cheating on their partners? Better hope no-one recognized you there!"

"Huh. If someone saw me, then I wonder what they were doing there. Were they meeting someone themselves?" Ruth began to cry. "You called me stupid! Oh Mark, this is awful! I didn't mean to do anything wrong, and I guess I was kind of stupid not to think it through. I wanted to know about Eleanor! But please, let's not fight about it. Is there any way for me to fix things?"

"Come here" Mark pulled her onto the sofa with him and hugged her tight. Zoe jumped up and tried to join in the embrace, worried blue eyes softening as Ruth cried on Mark's shoulder and they soothed one another gently. "So, did you learn anything about Eleanor?"

"Terrible things. She is in dreadful trouble with the Indonesian authorities, and the US government can't do much." Mark listened as she related the story George Stewart had told her, concluding tearfully "I just can't imagine how she is feeling now, and as for her husband — he truly needs some support. What a horrible situation! Did she need money so much that she had to do such a wicked thing?"

"I don't know the answer to that. I can't understand why she would risk everything for money. Maybe her gambling habits were out of control. Or perhaps that Radu guy was putting pressure on her for more money, who knows?"

"Next time you travel, please take me with you, Mark! I hate being left behind. It's lonely here. I have something else to tell you too. I don't know why I seem to be attracting trouble lately." Ruth, carefully editing out any reference to George Stewart and his advances, told Mark about her encounter with Nina Smirnova at the nursery.

"DON'T CALL HER, RUTH" he shouted. "You don't want to get mixed up in some Soviet games. You know how they play after our years in Moscow! Stay clear of it. Give me that piece of paper."

"No. I won't. Don't give me orders! She gave it to me, and I intend to think about how to handle it myself. She's a lovely warm person, not at all what you might expect of the wife of a high Soviet official."

Mark, exasperated and disbelieving Ruth's rebelliousness, stormed out. She heard Muhammad start the car and leave, presumably taking Mark to the office. Unless, she thought spitefully, he was going to Sunda Kelapa to meet someone. Well, I'm certainly not bored now, nor am I just doing what I am told like a good little foreign service wife. Maybe George has a point, and I do need to exert myself more. I think I will call Helke. She's sympathetic to Nina and maybe she can help me decide what to do. But I won't mention George. That would need too much explanation.

The telephone rang before she could call Helke. Gwen on the line said "Hi, Ruth! Just wanted to see if I could drop by for a minute right now, if it's convenient."

"Oh, that would be fine, Gwen. Just give me a few minutes to freshen up." As she combed her hair and attempted to remove traces of tears, she wondered why on earth Gwen was calling her out of the blue? She hadn't seen her for a couple of days though, so it would be good to catch up and she could talk to Helke tomorrow. Gwen's car was in the driveway already, and she rushed in, as usual talking as she entered. "Ruth, have you lost your mind? Why did you go to Sunda Kelapa with George Stewart, of all people? Phones are ringing all over Jakarta! What were you thinking?"

"Judging by your reaction, not to mention Mark's, I wasn't thinking at all. I went for lunch, nothing more, nothing less. Just lunch! But you might tell me why you're so rude about this, and how you know so fast that I had lunch with George."

"It's all over the city. Everyone is talking about that pretty little Mrs. Fairchild, seen lunching *à deux* at the World's End Hotel with George Stewart."

"It wasn't a hotel. It was a little restaurant above Pasar Ikan."

"That's the hotel restaurant. You must have gone up the outside stairs."

"How do you know about the restaurant and the outside stairs?" Ruth paused for a moment, feeling obliged to be polite, despite Gwen's provocation. "Gwen, it has been a long day! Lunch was pleasant, George was pleasant too, we walked around the market a little, then he told me about Eleanor's situation, and we came home. Mark's mad at me — called me stupid and rushed off to the office, and I feel terrible. How would I know about the red-light district unless someone told me? And nobody did, so I didn't know."

"But why did you have lunch with him?"

"Because I wanted to know about Eleanor, and he said he would tell me if I had lunch with him. I thought it would be alright — lunch is lunch, but evidently it's more than that here."

"If it's with George Stewart and you're a married woman, it is! Look, it'll blow over — I'll spread the word that you didn't know about Sunda Kelapa, and you will look silly for a while but it will be alright. So now, what's the story on Eleanor?"

Suddenly Ruth felt that Gwen's avid interest in the situation was unpleasant, and decided not to continue to discuss it with her. "I'm not free to tell you anything right now, Gwen, and I'm really tired. Let's put this off for today. Thanks for coming by, but I think I will rest for a while." Gently but firmly, she opened the door for Gwen and said goodbye courteously but distantly. Gwen, looking disappointed, left, although saying she would call tomorrow. Ruth began to wonder if she had made a mistake in trusting Gwen so easily; was she sincerely concerned with the situation at the post or was she a sensation-seeking rumormonger? She had been the first to give warning that all was not well, although that could be explained by her seeking information and opportunities for gossip.

When Gwen had gone, Ruth went to the phone and dialed the number given her in the note from Nina. To the woman who answered, she said "This is Ruth Fairchild. I have a message for Nina Smirnova. Please ask her if she could meet me and my friend Helke Ramsey for lunch one day soon. Ask her to name the day and place, please, and let me know at this phone number."

Then, she called Helke and invited her to tea at 4 o'clock, reflecting ruefully that perhaps it would also be a mistake to trust Helke. Be careful, she admonished herself, and don't say anything about George, best that his approaches be kept to yourself to make sure the gossip mill doesn't start grinding away again. Shakespeare warned — *"Friendship is constant in all things, Save in the office and affairs of love."* And while this isn't love, I suppose it's the kind of situation people find titillating — the possibility of a "love affair" or just a plain old adulterous "affair" would certainly add a twisty piquant tendril to the grapevine.

Chapter Eighteen

Nina Comes into Focus

The noise of the city was remote, and only the calls of birds could be heard clearly as Ruth and Helke walked toward the small white building which had been chosen by Nina Smirnova as the meeting place for their lunch.

The path from the parking area to the cafe wound through lush green lawns, sometimes past groups of tall palms and vivid flower beds, sometimes below wide-spreading shade trees or next to calm dark pools of water. Lotuses filled some of the curving pools, leathery green leaves held above the water's surface, with their pink flowers standing higher above. The water in other ponds was almost covered by the great flat leaves of tropical water lilies, 3-foot-wide green trays stable enough for small birds to walk and green frogs to perch while hunting for insects.

"It's amazing! Have you been here before, Helke?" asked Ruth, almost overwhelmed by the beauty of the garden, but mostly by the noontime heat and stifling humidity. "What are those things hanging in that big tree? They look like broken black umbrellas!"

"They're flying foxes — fruit bats — they wake at dusk and fly off to raid the orchards." replied Helke. "I've only been here a couple of times. We've stopped sometimes on our way up to Puntjak Mountain. The gardens were established by the Dutch in the early 19th century — trust Dutchmen to build a garden!"

"Cafe Taman Indah" — Beautiful Garden Cafe — read the sign on the little white building, and they entered a small restaurant on a covered verandah overlooking a lotus pond. Only a few tables were occupied; piquant aromas came from somewhere behind the screens at the end of the room, and a barefoot waiter in a white uniform ran out to greet them and show them to a table. Although Nina Petrovna had established the time and place, there was as yet no sign of her, and Ruth and Helke had a few minutes to look at their surroundings. "I think this must be where Solange saw Nina and Paul together at lunch" Ruth murmured to Helke. "I wonder if her husband knows about that."

Helke laughed "well, he may not know about that particular event, but they were totally indiscreet in Paul's garden, and I told you I thought someone was watching there. She's quite a lot younger than her husband, and maybe he's suspicious."

"Older men, younger wives — suspicion is part of the deal, isn't it?" Ruth said. "Maybe Paul got caught in a honey trap, using Nina as bait to catch him in indiscretions in order to compromise him. Somehow I think that's unlikely though; she's too well known, but I suppose she could have been forced into it."

Reflections from the water glimmered on the shadowed walls, and the room seemed to wait quietly. Dark polished wood floors, the ubiquitous slow-turning ceiling fans, potted palms in casual groups around the room, tables covered with white cloths and spaced widely apart — all together gave a sense of welcoming expectancy in the airy space. This is how it must have been fifty years ago, thought Ruth, before World War II when the colonial government was still confidently in power. Like Dutch art, there was nothing showy about the room; it expressed perfectly the Dutch love of solid domestic comfort, and gave no hint of any dawning awareness of the rise of nationalism in their colony that would eventually result in the loss of the power and wealth the Netherlands had drawn from it.

Suddenly, Nina was there, elegant as ever in a short pale blue linen dress with embroidered butterfly sleeves, her hair caught back by a batik scarf, a heavy white jade bracelet on her slim wrist. Her Indonesian companion, an older woman, wore traditional Indonesian silk batik *kain* and lace *kebaya*. As Helke and Ruth began to rise to greet them, Nina gestured that they should stay seated and introduced her companion. "May I present Annisa, my dear friend who helps me every day? Annisa, this is Ruth, who I met at the nursery, and her friend Helke, who I have not yet met." Ruth introduced Helke, saying only "Helke is a friend of mine, and a serious lover of dance. She recognized you when we saw you in the audience at the recent gamelan performance." They sat down, and the barefoot waiter arrived silently to present them with menus.

The food offered was Indonesian, simple and delicious—fresh fish and shrimp, chicken *satay, bami goreng,* and salads of fresh fruit and vegetables. The ladies placed their orders for light food with *kopi susu* — iced coffee — to drink. Nina began the conversation: "Helke, do you have special favorites among the dance traditions?"

Helke, a bit embarrassed at being asked this question by one of the best-known Russian dancers of recent years, answered carefully "Well, my tastes are pretty wide — I love classical ballet, also Martha Graham and the modern movement, and since being in Indonesia, I've become very interested in the Balinese and Javanese traditional dance too."

Nina smilingly said "Classical ballet is my discipline, and Annisa knows all about Balinese and Javanese dance. She has studied both of them for most of her life, and now she teaches and arranges performances. It was Annisa who produced the performance you saw at the *Hotel des Indes.*"

"Nina is much too generous to me" said Annisa, in clear and charmingly-accented English "I was born in Bali, and was chosen as a *legong* dancer in the sultan's palace when I was six. I moved to Jogjakarta with my parents when I was ten, and joined the palace group there. Not sure how much studying we did, it was mostly performing and having fun, like little kids do. Later though I was away from Indonesia for most of the year, at school in Europe. After I finished school, I met my husband when he was Indonesia's ambassador to France, and eventually we came home to live."

"Tell them about the festival you're arranging in Bali, Annisa!" Nina urged.

"Oh, it's exciting! A jet airport has just opened in Bali at Denpasar, and people from all over will be able to bypass Jakarta and arrive in Bali direct from all over the world! I am leading a group of dancers and enthusiasts to organize a festival of Balinese, Javanese, and European classical dance, and Nina has consented to dance there. We're hoping for international sponsorship, perhaps from Australia and the United States."

"That sounds wonderful!" said Helke "Maybe Ruth and I can manage to be there. I hear there are a couple of new hotels opening also."

"This will certainly put Bali on the world scene" remarked Ruth "Nina, do you know what you are going to dance? And how costumes, music, etc. will be managed? It will be complicated, I'm sure."

Nina broke in "Ruth, I don't know whether you know that Paul Faber and I were good friends. Before he disappeared, he had promised to help us to make contacts with wealthy people who might be interested in contributing. I know your husband replaced him in the embassy, and I hoped that you and he might be interested in taking a role also. It would mean a great deal if the United States were to be involved!"

Ruth, feeling devious and dishonest because she was concealing her knowledge of Paul and Nina's relationship but not willing yet to be honest, said "Oh, I would have to talk to Mark about that, and I am sure it needs go higher in the embassy, but tell me — what do you know about Paul's disappearance? It seems strange, mysterious, doesn't it?" Helke sat silent, seemingly frozen in place, while Annisa and Nina sat quietly absorbing this unexpected reaction from Ruth.

At last, Annisa said "That's a very dangerous beach. Many people have drowned there in the past. I don't know why the group went swimming there at night—it was crazy to do that."

Nina's eyes shone with tears and her voice trembled as she replied to Ruth "I know no more than you, but of course I am filled with suspicion. Paul and I were ..." she broke off as the waiter arrived with their food, and seemed to use the time to compose herself. Straightening her shoulders and lifting her head, she sat quietly waiting till he had finished before continuing "Paul loved music and dance; he was knowledgeable about it, and it drew us close as friends ..." she paused, searching for words "Now that he's gone, there is a problem ... and I miss him terribly."

Annisa reached out and covered Nina's hand on the table with her hand, and whispered something to her friend. "No!" cried Nina "I must trust someone! I need help, now that Paul is gone. It doesn't matter now what happened to him, just that he is gone and will never come back. I want to carry out our plans as far as possible, and I need the help of your embassy, Ruth."

Helke and Ruth sat still and silent. What can one say, thought Ruth? This is way above my level of understanding of diplomatic affairs, and Mark would tell me to get up right now and leave. Helke is probably thinking the same thing, and wishing she had never met me! But Helke, apparently made of strong practical stuff, said "Well, how can we help? If we are going to do anything, we need to know what the problem is."

"I want to be in the ballet world again, and my husband won't let me. I am almost too old to dance now, but I want to create and teach. Paul and I were planning to go to the United States together— perhaps you've guessed that we were more than friends—but now, without him, I don't know how to do it. Can you help me?"

Chapter Nineteen

Defection?

There was a long silence at the table as the ladies contemplated Nina's announcement. At last Ruth broke the silence. "It's called 'defecting' You wouldn't be the first dancer to leave the Soviet Union that way. Alexander Kuragin defected in 1962."

Nina, speaking softly, said "Defection. Yes, it is an ugly word! I've heard it applied to traitors. I just want to be free to use my body and my talent to do what I love best — to dance, and if I can no longer dance, then to teach and create works which allow me to take an audience with me on a journey into music and imagination. I want to follow Sasha to the West."

She's right, thought Ruth, it is an ugly word. It means to desert something or someone, perhaps to betray. Would Nina be considered a traitor by her compatriots if she were to leave her husband and refuse to return to her country? Could a dancer, an emblem of her country's love of beauty and culture, be called traitorous for that?

Ruth, answering but still preoccupied with the question of defection and its possible effect on Nina, said "Sasha has been very successful in the West, dancing with the most prestigious companies and partnering *prima ballerinas*, but I wonder how he is thought of in Russia by his colleagues and audiences. But is that important to you to be well thought of by your previous colleagues, Nina?"

Pausing for a long moment, Nina answered "More important than that for me is that my family — my mother and sister — are still there, and I am afraid they will be punished because of me, although there is hope that won't happen.

"I knew Sasha a little in Moscow. I never partnered with him — he was a star there, and I was too young and junior for that honor. He was an *enfant terrible*, incredibly talented but wild, untamable..." She shook her head, smiling a little at the memory, and went on "and I think his success in the west has made him even wilder! His family members were forced to write him letters begging him to come back. They complied, and so far, they haven't received drastic punishment. But he defied the authorities, and I must too. Whatever happens, I won't go back, and I'm going to leave my husband. I can't stay with him now in any case."

"But what will you do?" Helke asked "If you leave him, how will you live? Where will you go?"

Annisa reached out to take Nina's hand, saying to Helke "I will take care of her, and protect her as much as possible. I have connections in the Indonesian government who will help." Then, turning toward her friend "Nina, I think you need to trust these ladies and tell them the whole story."

As she watched Nina struggle with the decision to confide in her and Helke — two foreigners, strangers to her, from a country she had been taught all her life was the enemy--Ruth thought again that her physical beauty was striking. Even at such a painful time, she carried herself lightly, her head erect and poised, her heart-shaped face showing wide Slavic cheekbones below slightly tilted eyes — an exotic face, catlike, with an innocence that made it movingly lovely.

At last, she said "Alright. I will begin at the beginning, ten years ago when I met my husband. He was fifty-five, thirty years older than me, and a survivor of Stalin's purges. His career in the Ministry of Foreign Affairs was in full bloom, and I was dazzled by the prospect of overseas travel — not easy for Soviet citizens even now, but very difficult in those days. I suppose he wanted a wife who would be decorative and would help his career. Even in Soviet times, there is cachet in marrying a dancer from one of the great companies. At first, it was fine—not much love between us, only a kind of polite affection, but it was enough. I continued to dance at the Kirov, working my way up to soloist and getting some international recognition.

"A couple of years after we married, he was assigned to an English-speaking country in Africa — that is where I perfected my English. Although I wasn't truly happy, I was at least content with the novelty of life abroad. It was a small embassy, the government of the host country was Soviet-leaning and the climate was warm, so life was pleasant and I was able to find a ballet studio where I could continue my class routine with barre and floor work; for a dancer, the daily discipline of class is exhausting but comforting too."

She stopped for a moment for a sip of water, and to give her time to compose herself, Annisa said "I've always envied the classical dance custom of daily class, using a piano and accompanist. Do you need anything, Nina? I know this is hard for you!"

"No, now that I've begun, it's easier!" she replied, smiling a little and patting Annisa's arm. "So. After a couple of years there, he was transferred to Jakarta as ambassador, and suddenly everything changed. He became cold, stern, and remote. I assumed he was feeling the weight of his ambassadorial responsibilities, and I asked him how I could help. He rebuffed me abruptly. New 'security' officials arrived at the embassy, and I was confined to the residence for a long time without being told why. One day I was called into a dark little office and told by one of these 'security' officials that I would now be required to work on behalf of the Soviet government and that if I refused, my family in Leningrad would be severely punished by the withdrawal of their *propiska*, their permit to live in the city."

"I don't understand" cried Helke "People need a permit to live in Leningrad? And the government can take it away? Is that legal?"

Ruth and Nina spoke in unison: "Yes" — "Oh, Nina, excuse me" said Ruth "yes, people must have permits to rent apartments — Moscow and Leningrad are particularly desirable, for obvious reasons, and if their permit — their *propiska* —is withdrawn, legally they must be given another, but it will probably be for a less desirable region, perhaps far away from everything and everyone familiar to them. It was a common punishment, less so now but it still happens."

"She's right" Nina said "and I was terrified for my family. They would be lost outside of Leningrad, so I felt I had no choice— I had to agree." Her hands, lying on the table, were clenched together, the knuckles showing white with tension. Ruth, having lived for several years in Moscow, understood something of her dilemma.

Helke, though, had no experience of such practices and was sputtering with indignation. "That's immoral! People shouldn't be treated like that. But what did they want you to do for them? And did your husband know about this?"

"Poor Helke!" said Nina "This must seem barbaric to you. Yes, my husband knew about it, and had agreed before I learned about it.

"I was told that I must cultivate an American diplomat, and begin an affair with him. A meeting would be arranged — I would, of course, be the only one to know that it wasn't an accidental meeting. My purpose was to seduce this man into indiscretions which could be used to compromise him into becoming a Soviet asset. I was to be the bait in a 'honey trap'.

"In other words, I was to be a spy. And a prostitute."

Without waiting for comment from her audience, Nina continued. "I was dazed, confused, hurt. I went to my husband and asked him why this had happened. He laughed at me. He said 'Nina, we made a bargain, you and I, and now it's time to pay up. You didn't really expect to get all these privileges for free, did you? How naive you are!"

Talking faster now, and avoiding the eyes of her companions, she said "A meeting was arranged. A ticket to a dance performance was purchased for me. I don't know how it was done, but I was seated next to Paul Faber. I struck up a conversation — he didn't know who I was, and I identified myself simply as Nina, a former dancer. To my surprise, I liked him. We talked, flirted, laughed together. He invited me to join him for dinner the next night. We met at a simple restaurant in the old town, and talked for hours. He asked to see me again; I gave him Annisa's phone number, and her address. I took an embassy car to her place, he picked me up in his car, we went to dinner at his house, we made love, and I began to understand for the first time what it means to fall in love."

"A few days later, I made the decision to confess, tell him everything — who I was, that I was a spy, a provocateur— and ask him to trust me. I was scared he would denounce me, but I discovered that my love was returned. No longer alone, we made our decisions, planning for a future together. Strangely, because I was tasked with entrapping him, I suddenly had a great deal more freedom of movement than before. Now, I could go where and when I pleased, although I had to report daily what I was doing. It wasn't hard to invent activities! I was even allowed to fly to Singapore for a medical appointment, something that had never been allowed before. He joined me there, and it was marvelous. I held onto my passport from that trip, instead of returning it to security."

Suddenly her expression changed and she said "Annisa, we need to leave now. Ruth, Helke — I will be in touch." She and Annisa left the table and walked quietly and quickly toward the kitchen area and disappeared behind the screen, leaving Ruth to realize that that was how they had arrived so suddenly in the room earlier. She became aware that there were more people in the room than there had been when they arrived; riveted by Nina's telling of her story, she and Helke hadn't noticed that the restaurant had become busier. An arriving group was being greeted by the barefoot waiter, and conducted to a table near theirs.

"Hello, Ruth! Hi, Helke!" called Gwen from the nearby table as the new group settled in. "I'm surprised to see you here — I didn't know you knew it. Isn't it charming? A perfect place for a rendezvous, don't you think? George says it's one of his favorite places", indicating George Stewart among the group, along with Belinda and Joe Forrest. Bloody hell, thought Ruth. Now what?

Chapter Twenty

Ruth and Mark at Home

"Well!" Ruth said, as she and Helke rode in the car behind Muhammad on the way home "Do you think any of that group recognized Nina? And if so, will this be an item on the grapevine tonight?"

"I think she was gone so quickly that it would have been hard for anyone to recognize her. And if they did, why is it important? She and Annisa were simply trying to interest us in their Bali dance project" Helke replied. "At least, that's what we can say if anyone asks."

"Mmmm, I suppose so, but that was a nasty crack from Gwen about 'a perfect rendezvous', especially in front of George Stewart." Too late, she realized that Helke didn't know about her indiscreet lunch with George.

Helke, however, didn't seem to notice what Ruth had said and continued "... and the Bali project is interesting, don't you think? If Nina really does want to defect and goes through with it, the festival would give her some recent good publicity and remind people in the dance world of her career. She's been out of sight for quite a while now."

As Muhammad pulled the car into Helke's drive, Ruth said "thank you so much for coming with me today! Let's talk tomorrow. Now I have to go home and tell Mark about all this. Not sure how he's going to react!"

Helke got out, gave Ruth a grin, and said "well, maybe don't include the bit about George Stewart!" and Ruth realized that she knew about the lunch and was amused. Mortifying, she thought. How could I have been so stupid? And now, I have to face Mark with this story about Nina and her plans to defect, when he told me not to get involved. This is not going to be fun.

"Let's go home, Muhammad." Might as well get this over as soon as possible. Mark won't be home yet, and I will have time to rest a bit and freshen up. I'll make sure there's something special for dinner too, and a well-chilled bottle of wine—can't hurt, might help.

When she walked in the door, Muriarti told her that Mark had already been home but had gone for a walk, saying he would be back for dinner. Grateful for the additional time, she showered and changed clothes, then settled with Zoe on the screened porch to plan her campaign. Suddenly, Mark was there, asking "Just what do you think you are doing, Ruth? We need to talk, and it better be honest on your part."

Zoe fled. Ruth stared at him. "I don't know what you're talking about! What have I done? I want to talk to you about something too, but I haven't done anything to provoke this attack! Can you sit down and start over, please, so we both know where we are and what we're talking about?"

"I mean your flirtation with George Stewart! You were seen in Sunda Kelapa, holding hands, talking intently. You told me it was nothing, an innocent lunch, but what I heard today was a lot more than that, and I want to know where I stand with you."

Realizing that a cold bottle of wine and a low-cut dress weren't going to improve this situation very much, Ruth said "Alright. I didn't want to tell you this. George propositioned me, tried to get me to go to bed with him. I didn't know how to get away; I was stuck down there without a way to get home. I knew I had been an idiot accepting his invitation to lunch, and I'd put myself into a mess with my naivety. I didn't think he would be so bold. I hoped that he would accept my refusal and that you wouldn't be hurt by knowing about it. That's all, I promise!"

"But you must have done something to encourage him! Men don't act that way unless there are hints that the woman is receptive to his approaches."

"Mark, I don't think George Stewart needs encouragement! He is accustomed to conquest, and seems to think that anyone is susceptible to his charm — he even boasts about it! He's a predator. And I was afraid that if I told you, it would make it difficult for you to work with him, and this embassy is complicated enough that I didn't want to add to your problems."

Mark had listened, and calmed down. "Well, I can't say I exactly understand, but I won't punch him in the jaw; I'm mad but there's not much I can do about it. We've always been honest with one another, and I trust you to tell me the truth." Ruth felt a pang when he said this, thinking of what she had to tell him about her meeting with Nina Petrovna.

But first, she thought, let's clear the air and get George Stewart out of the way.

"But what happened today? How did you hear about this? Or have you been stewing about it since last week, worrying?"

"Your friend Gwen called me at work this morning, wanting to know where you were so she could invite you to lunch— said she couldn't reach you at home. But I think she called to make sure I knew about your romantic date with Stewart. She was very solicitous — 'I think you ought to know ... Ruth is so innocent, so sweet ... She is such a good friend .... I am so fond of her ... I thought you ought to know so you could prevent her being hurt by getting involved with ...' "

"Oooh! What a '*good friend*' she is! I was mistaken in her, I must admit! She loves gossip and stirring up trouble. I think she's jealous of any other friends I have — she doesn't like Helke, I know. Well, forewarned is forearmed." Zoe, sensing a change in the emotional weather, padded back, ready for a little lap time and Mark called out to Siti to bring their evening drinks. They sat quietly for a while, listening to the late afternoon sounds, Zoe's purr making a soft counterpoint to the melodic call to prayer from the mosque and the rhythmic calls of the passing street vendors.

Ruth decided that the time was right to tell Mark about her lunch with Nina. "Mark, I have something else I need to talk with you about too. You'll probably be mad, but I hope we can work things out. I had lunch today with Nina

Smirnova and an Indonesian friend of hers. Helke Ramsey was with us also. It was an interesting .... "

Mark broke in "I told you not to contact her after you met her at the nursery. Why did you do this? Don't you have any sense? And we have just been talking about trust!"

"Mark, you can't tell me what to do. If you respected me, you wouldn't do that. It isn't fair— you are saying that you are the boss, the decision maker in this relationship, and that I have no freedom. That might have worked for your parents' generation, but it won't work now! We need to work together, make decisions together — that's the only way to stay together and be happy. I'm your wife, not your servant."

Zoe left the room again, tail fluffed out. "I called Nina because I liked her. I wanted to see her again. I loved Moscow, and I was attracted to her because of my happy memories of Russia, by her charm, and my love of classical ballet. She was part of that world, and I wanted to be in touch with a little piece of it."

"You were clueless. You don't know anything about the rules of diplomacy, and the fine tuning of contacts between diplomats who represent their countries' foreign policies You could do a great deal of damage, blundering in."

"How? Apparently, wives are just for ornament anyway. Arrogance doesn't suit you, Mark."

"Sarcasm suits you even less, Ruth."

"Truce, Truce!" called Mark after a moment or two "let's see if we can talk about this without getting het up!"

Simmering, Ruth said "Helke and I had lunch with Nina and her friend Annisa today—Annisa's husband was Indonesia's ambassador to France a few years ago and she's got all kinds of connections. They are organizing a dance festival in Bali in a couple of months, and they'd like the embassy to take part. It's a cultural event. Is there something wrong with that?"

"Well, I can't see what is so terribly important about it — but I can see that a dance festival could be new and different, and that perhaps the cultural section would be interested in figuring out a way to work with Nina and her group. I can certainly talk to the embassy about it. Would that help?"

"Yes, it would. But there's something else that dawned on me when I was listening to Nina's story about her relationship with Paul. She told us something important, much more important than a dance festival. I think I know what Paul Faber wanted to discuss with the top officials of the embassy. He died before he could talk to them."

Ruth related to Mark the story she and Helke had heard from Nina about her meeting with Paul and their subsequent love affair, with all its complications. "I may not be sophisticated in security matters, but even a mere wife can see that there are questions here that need to be answered. I believe she was telling the truth ..."

"Ruth, you and I need to talk to the security people at the embassy right now. This is way above our decision-making level!"

"No. You can do that you want to, but I won't. She trusts me, I believe her story, and I won't let her down. This can be handled on a personal basis, I'm sure. And if you go to security, I will deny everything."

"Right!" yelled Mark. "We can all get together and sing 'It's a Small World After All', and everything will be lovely! Wake up, Ruth! The wife of a Soviet ambassador is going to defect with the help of a couple of American foreign service wives, and we're all going to live happily ever after? If you believe that, I've got a bridge to sell you!"

Chapter Twenty-one

Reflections

The morning sun spilled onto the dining porch where Mark and Ruth sat breakfasting in strained silence. The flower vendor bicycled up, waving cheerfully at Ruth, one of his best customers. The panniers on his cycle overflowed with flowers — red, yellow and orange orchids, pink and purple asters, scented lilies, tall spires of ginger, and tropical flowers with exotic shapes and names unknown to Ruth. He delivered her usual order and promised to return later in the day with some new blooms. Grumpily Mark said "Don't we have enough flowers yet? This place looks like a bootlegger's funeral."

Deciding not to take issue with that comment, Ruth answered "well, they help to cheer up the place until we get our own things. It's a bit dreary with no pictures, no curtains, just this generic beige furniture, don't you think?"

"I like beige." Mark paused, then said

"Are you coming to the embassy with me this morning to talk to security?"

"Why? I have things to do here. Muriarti is giving me a lesson in Indonesian cooking later." She left the table and went to join Zoe in front of the big bird cage, where the little flock of brightly colored budgerigars were chirping and perching contentedly. In the small universe of the cage, couples formed, dissolved, reformed casually; blue feathers with green today, tomorrow yellow with the blue;

how do they choose, wondered Ruth. Do they worry about responsibility, or promises? Have they a sense of the future, or do they simply enjoy what comes their way? Zoe, intent on the fluttering birds, chattered her teeth softly from time to time as if she could feel her prey in her mouth. Do they understand that Zoe is an effective predator despite her soft prettiness and lambent blue eyes, and that she has sharp teeth and claws with which she could —and would— hurt them?

Pulled back from her reflective distance, she heard Mark saying "Ruth, we must talk to security about this whole Nina Smirnova thing. If the press got hold of it, it would be a huge scandal and would probably result in Nina being sent back to the Soviet Union in disgrace. Can you see that if we tell security and get their help, it's going to be much better for all involved?"

Ruth, who had been mulling things over during the night, was prepared now to accept that help was needed although she still had reservations. "I suppose you're right. But I am not prepared to just turn it over to a couple of CIA guys — I've met some of the local station officers, and they impress me as lacking subtlety. I think we should hold out for Helke and me to be the front people, but accept advice and help from embassy security when needed."

Surprised at the overnight sea change, Mark asked "What about the cultural section? How would you feel about working with them? They are used to dealing with artists and traveling shows, and they'd be able to be pretty helpful with the dance festival. I think they could work easily with security."

"I suppose so, if it could be worked out. So, where do we start? We need to move pretty quickly, I think, before someone gets wind of it and the gossip begins. I told you about Gwen and her little lunch party yesterday — they probably saw Nina and Annisa leaving our table."

Mark thought for a while, before saying "Let me talk to security this morning and feel things out. This is going to have to go to Washington, and I'm sure they will want to talk to you and Helke, and pretty soon too, so be ready to come down to the embassy later today." He stood up from the table, saying "It's time to go. I'll call you when I have any news." and walked to her, enclosing her in his arms and saying softly "I'm sorry. I'll try to be more aware of your feelings; I know I have a lot to learn. Peace? Hey, you're still in your pajamas — let's go back to bed for a little bit!"

"Mmmm, no. You need to get to the office! But let's have an early night tonight. And peace, of course! I'm sorry to be such a prickle sometimes."

Mark shouted for Muhammad and left, calling out "I'll send Muhammad back with the car later. And I really like the flowers. They look more like a bootlegger's wedding than a funeral."

Laughing, Ruth walked into the house, intending to go with Muriarti to the market for the supplies needed for her Indonesian cooking lesson. As she passed the telephone, it began to ring and she picked it up. "Mrs. Fairchild, this is Nini in the admin section. I wanted to let you know that your household goods shipment came in last night, and it's on the truck on the way to your house right now."

Well, there goes my day, thought Ruth as she headed to the bedroom to get dressed. Work clothes, definitely. I wish women could wear blue jeans, it would be so practical; Lord, I can imagine what Belinda would say if I showed up in jeans sometime "Ruth, ladies don't wear dungarees. They are the garb of laborers. We must remember our position here."

The sound of boxes being dumped helter-skelter into the living room made her run out, to find Siti and Muriati attempting to direct the workers. "Wait! wait! We need the packing list, so we know where these things go. Where is George Stewart, when he could be useful?" At that moment, she saw George exiting an embassy car in the driveway and approaching the front door. "Hi, George! We need the packing list — do you have it? I want to check that everything is here."

"Relax, Ruth! I've got the list, and I'm going to help you check everything in." Suddenly, he became an impressive masculine presence, giving orders in Indonesian in a strong, quiet voice, sorting the chaos of boxes into organization, setting servants and workmen to careful industry as they moved boxes to their appropriate places and began to unpack them. He certainly does a hands-on job as admin officer, thought Ruth. Surely, he doesn't do this for every new staff person.

Pieces of the Fairchilds' life in Paris began to appear from the boxes. A framed map of the Paris Metro, a copy of "Mastering the Art of French Cooking", a French press for coffee, a stone reproduction of the Winged Victory, recalling the original so dramatically poised for flight at the top of the Louvre stairs, a small table of holly wood with a marble top and ormolu trimmings, a French-English dictionary and a well-thumbed book of French irregular verbs, two brass lamps with silk shades, pieces of ceramic cookware, pots and pans, cheese trays, silverware and French china. George called out "Ruth, how many silk damask pillows do you need? This box has about a dozen. Plus silk draperies, and feather quilts! Perfect for Paris — bet they'll be really useful here on cold foggy nights!"

Amusedly watching him, Ruth felt again the appeal of his personality and a certain attraction that she had felt during their lunch in Sunda Kelapa. To escape, she went to the kitchen to prepare a tray of coffee and lemonade for everyone. The kitchen was quiet and tidy, a calm contrast to the bustle in the rest of the house and she began to relax her guard. Surely George will behave appropriately today right here in my home. Muriarti came in and took the tray of drinks, and Ruth remained there at the sink, clearing up and resting a little before returning to work.

George opened the door, saying as he entered "Oh, Ruth, there you are. I've been looking for you. What were you doing up at Bogor with Nina Smirnova yesterday? Gwen and I were wondering how you met her. Striking woman, that Nina!" Watching him close the door behind him, she was reminded of Zoe in front of the bird cage. He has the same look of the predatory feline studying its prey, calculating the actions needed to catch it, anticipating with relish the struggles before the kill and the eventual taste of triumph. He walked over to where she stood at the sink, putting his arms around her and kissing her hard, a deep kiss that left her with little doubt of his intentions. To her dismay, Ruth felt her body respond to him. She pulled away and ran from the room.

Chapter Twenty-two

The Banyan Tree

Ruth ran out of the kitchen and left the house without telling anyone where she was going. Distraught, upset by the event in the kitchen, she needed time and privacy to reflect on George Stewart's move and her own response.

The day was heating up, and she would need a hat and a parasol if she were to walk anywhere. The deep shade of the banyan tree at the corner of the street drew her eye; she could sit unnoticed at the little coffee stall under the tree for a while among the chess and card players who were there every day. Mark was always saying he wanted to sit there and play a chess game with one of the regulars, but so far, he didn't ever seem to have enough free time to do so.

The group of men looked surprised when she appeared, but the stallholder courteously offered her a wobbly chair and she sat down at a little table, attempting to fade into the shadows and sit unnoticed while she tried to arrange her thoughts. A young boy brought coffee for her — the owner of the stall pointed to her house and nodded, indicating that he knew her by sight and would wait for his money—and the chess players returned to their games.

It was pleasant in the shade. The great tree rustled and whispered around her with its own life and calm presence. Shafts of sun filtered through the leaves, and the aerial roots dropping down from the branches to the ground reminded her of the reeded columns in European cathedrals. They formed small areas of enclosure, giving a sense of seclusion to where she sat. She had read that Indonesians believe that banyan trees are places of peace and temporary refuge for the spirits of the dead as they leave the living world and face their journey into eternity. I'm not leaving the living world, thought Ruth, but I certainly need some peace in my life right now. What to do about George Stewart? And why can't I manage to discourage him finally? Is it because I am attracted to him? I don't want to be, I want things to go back to where they were before— simple, uncomplicated, ordinary. Is it the place, the tropical climate, the incredible vitality of the vegetation, relationships seeming to intertwine and tangle like the exuberant vines?

Her thoughts ran on and on ... Mark — what is happening with him? He has changed, and I don't know why. He says everything I do is wrong. Could there be someone else? But I have been lying to him telling him that my meeting with George was an innocent matter, and trying to make myself believe it too. It wasn't just lunch. I enjoyed it. I liked the attention of a handsome man, the fun of flirting with him, and the titillating prospect of a sexual encounter. So there, now I have admitted it. To myself anyway.

And Nina — how can I help her? She has Annisa and her other friends, but she has asked me for help because of my connection with the embassy. I feel a closeness to her because of Leonie and their mutual love for ballet, and I would like to be her friend. She is going to want every bit of assistance we can find. She needs money, contacts in the US, a visa — a plan! Do we depend on official help or do we try to pull this off ourselves? Is it more likely that the

Soviets will learn about it from us, or from security? They probably have a source in the embassy—I would be very surprised if they don't! But if we keep our group small, we should be able to avoid their learning about Nina's intention to defect until we can get her safely away.

We have Nina, Annisa and her contacts, Helke, and me. Could Mark be convinced to join us? I hope he will, but I think his essential belief in the rightness of US policy will stop him, and if I use him for what help he can give us without being honest with him, my marriage will be over. Is that what I want? Who else could be included? Gwen? No, she's too fond of gossip. Belinda Forrest? Oh, please! George Stewart? Too dangerous! But ... maybe. He seemed sympathetic when he told us about Paul's will and he has a lot of information. I wonder where he gets it. But —- can I handle him? Is there a way to control him, short of getting into bed with him? And would even that make him controllable?

She began to think about the whole picture of her experiences in Jakarta; such a short time for so much to have happened, and so many questions without answers. What really happened to Paul Faber? Who was Suleiman? What about the photos that George showed Gwen and me — the expensive watch Suleiman was wearing when he was found floating in the pool? And the one of him outside the Soviet ambassador's residence? Is Nina telling the truth? Why was she lunching with Bernie Jackson, Eleanor's husband, at the Balinese restaurant that day that Gwen and I and the whole feminine expat community saw them? Was someone hiding in Helke's garden and watching Nina and Paul making love in his garden? Who? And why?

She had no answers, but her time in the quiet presence of the tree had helped to still the fears and worries that had bothered her for days now, and given her a new sense of purpose. She began to gather her things and stood up, preparing to leave her hiding place and go home.

As she did so, she saw George walk into the tree's shade. He called to her "Wait, Ruth! Can we sit down and talk for a minute? Please?" She sat down again, not wanting to make a scene in public, and watched while he paused to speak to the cafe owner. Pulling up another chair, he sat down and said "Well. So, this is where you went. Everyone's been looking for you for ages. We have to talk, you and I." The same small boy who had brought coffee to her came again, this time with bottled cold drinks and a little tray containing two *kretek* cigarettes and a tiny book of matches. "Durian soda, Ruth — very refreshing. And would you smoke a peace pipe with me?", indicating the cigarettes.

She shook her head but didn't speak, and he said "Don't look so scared. I don't usually bite", giving her a silly exaggerated leer and lighting a cigarette. The fragrant clove-scented smoke drifted into the branches as he said "Ruth, what I have to tell you is meant to be helpful, and I hope you will listen to me. First though, I am sorry I frightened you with my advances. I find you very attractive, and I think you're interested too." Laughing, he said "I guess it wasn't a very good time, right there in your kitchen! I won't promise not to try again at a better time, but for now there's something more important that we need to discuss."

"I will give you five minutes" Ruth said "and then I will leave. I will make a scene, if necessary, in order to get away. So, beginning to time it now .... "

"Thank you. Ruth, have you wondered how I have so much information about all the things that have been going on in this embassy in the two months since you and Mark arrived?" Without stopping for a response from her, he continued "My position as Administrative Officer here is my cover. I'm the head of the State Department security detachment on post. My deputy does the administrative office work. I know that Nina Smirnova has contacted you in the hope of getting some assistance with the dance festival in Bali and I am hoping that we can work together in order to get Nina safely out of Bali to the United States— something Paul Faber wanted very much for her, and for which he may have been killed."

"Wait a minute. What are you saying? You are helping Nina and encouraging me to get involved? And that Paul may have been murdered?"

"Yes, all correct. That's what I'm saying. We need to begin working on this as soon as possible. I have some ideas and, of course, some means to help to accomplish it."

"Can your deputy handle everything in the administrative realm? For instance, why were you at my house to help with our household stuff today?"

"Because I wanted a chance to talk to you. Sorry about the little surprise in the kitchen. I just couldn't resist when I saw you alone in there. Vickie Ormond, my deputy, is very competent; Mark enjoyed meeting her on the trip to Sumatra, and they have seen one another a few times since."

"She went to Sumatra with him, when I had to stay behind?"

"Oh, I'm sorry — didn't you know?"

"Are they having an affair?"

"I wouldn't call it an affair yet, more a blossoming friendship."

This time Ruth didn't run away.

Chapter Twenty-three

Peace?

The house was quiet when Ruth returned from the banyan tree cafe. George's car was gone, as was the delivery truck with the empty shipping container. Muhammad was polishing their car, the only vehicle in the driveway. As she walked up the path to the front door, she noticed how well the garden was developing under Sunardi's care, looking orderly and peaceful. The tiny lawn was neatly clipped, the hedge of bougainvillea was growing energetically and the bird-planted papayas were setting fruit fifteen feet up their skinny trunks. Ruth, with her love of green growing things, had yearned for something like this tropical garden. She recollected their tiny balcony in Moscow — too small for anything but a straight chair and one potted plant, although its view of the river and the Stalinist-style Hotel Ukraina compensated somewhat. And the minute and exquisite garden behind their Paris apartment, with its gravel paths and elaborate parterres was reserved for the landlord, tenants permitted only to look from above.

Now that we have our own things, she thought, maybe Mark and I can re-establish a home and find our routines again, and I can dig in the dirt. The journey from Paris to here was long, and we are both off balance. Perhaps his interest in Vickie is because she seems settled, peaceful, a sort of refuge. I am not going to say anything about her — not yet, anyway. Coming into a new assignment the way he has had to — stepping into someone else's position at short notice after a tragedy — has been very rough on him.

And, while a new post is exciting, it's also hard on daily life: new colleagues, new work responsibilities, local conditions. It takes time to find household needs — reliable dry cleaner, grocery store, school for the kids, the post office, a good bakery —while living with the generic government furniture chosen from a catalogue by bureaucrats in Washington and intended to suit quarters around the world; the same beige sofa, dining table, chairs, from Moscow to Montevideo, the limited stuff in the Welcome Kit — dented pots in mysterious sizes, either sized for a family of ten or suitable to boil one egg at most, three unmatched plates, one souffle dish, two forks, and three unmatched bedsheets of varying sizes. We've got our own *truc* now, and we can shut out Vickie and George and have a home together again.

As she entered the house, she saw that the boxes were gone and their contents were neatly but confusedly distributed everywhere around the rooms. "Ruth! Where have you been? I've been worried about you!" Mark said, from the dining room chair he had apparently cleared to sit on by piling its contents on the floor next to him. "George Stewart called me, to tell me our effects were in and that you were trying to handle the unpacking by yourself, so I came home but you were gone. I'm sorry — were you upset at being left to do it alone?"

"Oh, hi, Mark. Not really upset, just a bit overwhelmed. I left the crew to empty the boxes and went for a walk and a cup of coffee under the banyan tree at the corner" Ruth answered a bit coolly, carefully omitting George's involvement in anything. Maybe, she thought, Mark didn't know that he was here. And I am not going to mention Vickie. Don't mention Vickie, she instructed herself.

"Who is Vickie Ormond?" she asked. "And how did she get to go to Sumatra with the group when I couldn't go?" She started to cry. Today is too much — the quarrel with Mark about Nina yesterday and its shadow at breakfast, the sudden arrival of their household goods and the resulting chaos, the appearance of George in the kitchen and his abrupt escalation of his efforts at seduction, his reappearance in the little cafe under the banyan and the revelation about his true position in the embassy. And then the casual divulgence of Mark's "blossoming friendship" with Vickie Ormond. Once again, she ran out of the house, this time in tears.

Mark was right behind her. "Ruth! Wait! Hold on—let me get the car and we can go somewhere alone and talk! Don't go away, please!" She stopped, watching him run back and get the car from Muhammad, then drive toward her and stop so she could get in. "We're not going to talk until we can find a quiet place where we can look at one another and be honest" he said. "This has all gone too far."

Fifteen minutes later, Mark pulled the car onto the side of the road, at a place overlooking rice *padis*. A farmer was working a *padi* with his water buffalo, pulling a plough through the dried mud and muck of the drained field. There were honking querulous geese on the dykes between the *padi* fields, guarded by a boy wearing a large bamboo sunhat; huge spider webs hung from the electric wires above, and clouds of dragonflies zoomed and rocketed above the water. He turned toward her and said softly "Alright, Ruth. Time to talk now, don't you think?"

"Are you having an affair with Vickie Ormond?" Appallingly, he began to laugh and she started to cry again.

"Oh, I'm sorry, Ruth — I don't mean to be unkind! You haven't met Vickie. She's a lovely woman — kind, generous, reminds me of my gym teacher in sixth grade. Dresses like him too. Very earnest, very athletic, birdwatching at dawn, calisthenics to follow, raw carrots for snacks and oatmeal for breakfast. Not a bit like you, but I know you would like her!"

Ruth cried harder, from relief and the ease of tension. "George Stewart said you and she have a "blossoming friendship." I will kill him next time I see him."

"When did he say that?" Mark asked, handing her his handkerchief.

Drying her tears on the big square of white cloth (she noticed it was slightly frayed at the edge and had a betel nut stain; time to talk to Hindun, the laundress), she answered "When he came to the house this morning with our shipment. He helped a bit before I left the house."

"I didn't know he was there."

Editing carefully, Ruth said "It was nothing. He was helpful with the work crew." She moved into safer territory "But he told me something that I didn't know — did you know that he is State Department security, and the admin job is his cover?"

"Yes, I learned that today myself. Vickie's his deputy and does the admin stuff, poor woman! He and I talked briefly at the embassy — I saw him as soon as I got there; he is aware that Nina wants to defect and he's apparently willing to help get her out of Indonesia safely. That will make things much simpler." He paused for a moment, then went on "it will make it possible for me to help also. I didn't have time to talk to the cultural section this morning, but Stewart said he will do that and get them involved. But you and Helke will still have to talk to him and tell him the story you heard from Nina and Annisa. Can you do that?"

"Yes, if she and I can go together and you can come too."

"I'm sure that can be worked out. Now, let's see if we can get back to trusting one another." He began to laugh again "Oh, Ruth! You have to meet Vickie! She really is a pleasant woman, and fun to be with on a trip. Let's ask her to dinner, and if you are still jealous after you meet her, I'll buy us a trip to Bali."

Ruth cheered up. "A dinner party! That's a wonderful idea, and now we have our stuff and we don't have to use the welcome kit so we'll have enough plates. It could be a working event, doing some planning for the Bali dance festival. I'll cook French food, if I can get the ingredients here" — laughing at the unlikeliness of this — "do you think I can get Poulets de Bresse and butter from Normandy in the market?"

They sat silently, holding hands. Couples who are together for a long time, or those who have faced life-altering difficulties and managed to stay together, often seem able to communicate at a level deeper than speech. The afternoon began to cool and the shadows lengthened as their side of the earth turned away from the sun. The farmer and his buffalo left the field and the boy drove the hissing geese ahead of him toward the farmhouse that could be seen in the distance.

It was time to go home. Mark started the engine but shut it off after a moment and said "How far has it gone with Stewart, Ruth? Why aren't you being honest with me? I think I deserve that, at least."

Chapter Twenty-four

The Dinner Party

Night-scented jasmine and gardenia perfumed the dark garden, and small clay oil lamps outlined the path to the front door. A delicate chandelier contrived of candles and flowers, lightly trembling in the night breeze, hung over the door where Siti and Hindun, wearing their best lace blouses, jasmine flowers in their oiled black hair, waited to welcome the guests.

"Ruth, better hurry up! People will be here any minute." Mark called "I'm about finished setting up the bar."

In the dining porch, Ruth gave a last look at the dinner table and ran to the kitchen to check on the food preparation which Muriarti and a helper —her nephew, hired for the evening—were completing. Too bad about the plans for French food, thought Ruth, but this international blend of a menu would be interesting — Russian blini, tiny buckwheat pancakes, served with sour cream and red caviar (found, astonishingly, in a jar at Toko Sunlight), followed by giant shrimp, a local delicacy, in a creamy curry with ginger, a coconut rice cone and green papaya salad. Dessert—Napoleons, a French confection of crisp pastry with a lemon filling and crême Chantilly. Coffee, liqueurs and mosquito repellent would be served in the candlelit garden.

"I have to get dressed! I'll be out in a minute. Start serving drinks, if they get there before I do!" In the bedroom, she hastily brushed her hair and pulled it up into a fashionable high chignon jokingly called "Roman Empress", and stepped into a brief white silk shift with narrow pearl-beaded straps, cut high in front, daringly low in back, with silver sandals on her feet.

When she came out, Mark was lounging in a chair, smoking a cigarette. "That hairdo makes you look haughty and untouchable! New dress? Or is it lingerie—there's not much of it. Is this for me or Stewart?"

"You paid for it. You decide. I bought it in Paris, but I think it will be appreciated more here."

Mark flinched. No time now to take this up, Ruth thought. Probably just as well.

The Ramseys, Helke and her husband Howard, appeared from the darkness, to be greeted politely by Siti and Hindun, and passed to Mark and Ruth in the living room. Then another flurry of arrival, and Bernie Jackson, Eleanor's husband, appeared. Mark introduced him to Ruth, who said "I am really glad you could come. How is Eleanor? Any word on getting her out?"

"Still in jail" said Bernie gloomily "not much to be done except visit her when it's permitted. Conditions are terrible. I feel I have to stay in Jakarta to help her any way I can. Thanks for including me tonight—I don't get invited much anymore."

Annisa was next to arrive; Ruth welcomed her warmly and introduced her around, while Mark took care of drinks. Zoe arrived, sociably going from person to person in a feline ritual of welcome, and people began to chat easily.

"I wonder where Stewart is?" said Mark. "He asked if he could bring a guest." Just then, George Stewart walked in the door, escorting a stunning woman. Tall, slim, her very short blonde hair cut close to her head in feathery wisps, framing a strong, expressive face—Joan of Arc if she had lived to be thirty, Ruth thought. There was shrewdness and a touch of willfulness in her expression. She wore a simple, almost severe, cream linen shift, skillfully cut to subtly hint at the body beneath, very short to show gorgeous legs, and belted loosely at the hip with a gold chain. More striking than conventionally pretty, she needed no ornament but long gold earrings of Chinese design accentuated her features "Hey, Vickie!", Mark called "Stewart didn't tell me he was bringing you! This is great! Ruth, Ruth, come and meet Vickie Ormond!"

"Markie!" squealed this vision of delight "Long time no see—I sure have missed you!"

Well! Reminds him of his gym instructor, does she, thought Ruth. Who designed that dress though? I need the name! "It's lovely to meet you at last, Vickie. I've heard so much about you from Mark, and from George too. Mark will get drinks for you both, and then we will sit down at the dinner table."

"Why, thank you for includin' me, Ruth" Vickie said politely, in a broad Texas twang.

"Let's see" Ruth said as they arrived in the dining porch, pretending she needed to think about the seating "Annisa on Mark's right, Vickie on his left, Bernie on my right..." she continued, letting Mark have Vickie next to him, till all were seated. Too late she realized that she had accidentally seated George next to her. Well, sauce for the goose tonight too, she thought.

"Such delicious smells from the kitchen! A French menu tonight?" asked Helke.

"International" answered Ruth briefly "too hard to get French ingredients—cream and butter from tins aren't ideal!"

"I've never been to France" Vickie said. "My experience in the foreign service is limited to Asia, and my food tastes are embarrassin'ly healthy — raw vegetables, fish and all, but maybe someday I'll get a post in Europe and learn about French food!"

"Oh, I hope you will" Ruth purred "you would love France in so many ways. French men are very susceptible to American blondes!" I shouldn't have had that glass of wine while I got dressed, she realized.

Ruth and Mark had agreed to give the guests time to chatter while the first course was passed, before raising the topic of Nina and her problems but George spoke as soon as everyone was seated "I think you all know why we are here tonight — I suppose we could be called "Friends of Nina Petrovna." We need to form a plan to help her defect. I asked Vickie to join us—as acting admin person, she has a lot of practical know-how. First though, I think we should all know about Bernie's conversation with Nina a while back, when she approached him for help. He came to me with the story, and I'll let him tell it now."

Mark looked unhappy at having his host duties snatched away, but said nothing. Bernie, seeming tired and subdued, spoke quietly "I got a phone call one day from Annisa. She and I had met at the Jakarta Cultural Centre where I had taken some language lessons, and she asked if I would be kind enough to help a friend of hers with a visa problem."

Annisa nodded "Yes, since Bernie is the visa officer, he seemed like the right person to talk with, and we made an appointment for Nina to meet him at the Dewi Melanting restaurant."

"With hindsight, it wasn't the best place to meet!" Bernie continued "Every foreigner in Jakarta was there for lunch and recognized her; the grapevine was really hot that night! Anyway — we met, and she told me that she needs a visa for the United States, that she is in possession of a Soviet passport in her name, and that she is planning to visit friends in San Francisco."

"Do you have any discretion to issue her a visa, Bernie?" inquired Mark.

"Yes, up to a point. If I am convinced that she is only visiting the country, she can have a visitor's visa. Regulations say she must come to the embassy to get it, but since I am in charge of the section, it wouldn't be any real problem to fudge that requirement and for security reasons it would probably make sense. All kinds of things could happen if she were to stay in the US though" he paused for a moment and laughed sarcastically "but none of it would affect me so I would be willing to issue one. But because of who she is — wife of a Soviet ambassador —I had some security concerns, so I went to George Stewart."

Helke asked "Bernie, did you know at the time that Nina and Paul Faber had been having an affair before he disappeared?"

"No. But Stewart did, and told me about it. It wouldn't have made any difference to my decision about the visa though. And still won't."

There was a scuffle outside, a shout from Sunardi, the guard, running feet, the clang and scrape of the gate being opened. Stewart and Howard Ramsay ran out, and they could hear Sunardi explaining that he had found a man hiding in the bushes outside the porch, but couldn't identify him. "He's gone now. Just as well you have a guard" Howard said as the men re-entered. "Not much for us to do, but we probably shouldn't be talking about Nina here where it's easy to be overheard."

"Yeah" Mark agreed "Ruth, we should move inside."

"Can we have dinner?" Ruth pleaded "we can just talk about other things, and make a plan to talk somewhere more secure later. I would hate to waste our first dinner party here, and Muriarti has worked so hard on it!" The guests began to settle down again, Howard slid back into his chair and, looking down the table, she could see Mark and Vickie leaning close and smiling at one another. Probably playing footsie under the table, she thought. "Mark, can you pour more wine, please?" Turning to George, Ruth extended her hand — "George, come back and sit down. You deserve another glass of wine."

The main course was put in front of her to serve. "These shrimp are so delicious!", Ruth said, addressing the table at large. "Muhammad took me to Sunda Kelapa this morning to get them. I had lunch down there a couple of weeks ago, and I loved the old port and Pasar Ikan. The hotel restaurant there has excellent fish dishes too. I suppose there are other fascinating places in the archipelago — Sumatra must be incredible—but so far, Sunda Kelapa is my favorite."

There, she thought. A declaration of war. Let's see what Mark makes of that. A warm hand surreptitiously rubbing her bare back reminded her that George was seated next to her.

"Dessert and coffee in the garden, everyone. Sunardi will keep us safe from prowlers" Ruth said. "Insect repellent will take care of most other hazards."

Chapter Twenty-five

The Night Wind

The party adjourned to the garden, where dessert and coffee were laid out on a glass-topped table and big comfortable rattan chairs were arranged in a group, each with a small table close by. The night wind made the candles flicker and carried with it the delicate scent of Queen-of-the-night blooming in a neighborhood garden. The mosquito repellent was passed to those who needed it, the ladies flipped open their little fans, and people relaxed with their coffee and dessert. Conversation became easy in the darkness.

"Ruth, this is lovely." Helke said "a couple of months ago, there was nothing here but a mango tree, and now just look at it! It's almost magical—you have a gift for garden creation!"

"This was how Nina and Ruth met" chimed in Annisa "they were at a nursery, shopping for plants and Nina told me they encountered one another in the shade house." She continued quietly "Mr. Stewart, is it true that the cultural section of the US embassy is interested in being a sponsor of the dance festival, and that they have some leads on funding?"

"Annisa, please call me George! And yes, it's true. The details will take a while to work out though."

From her seat between Helke and George — carefully arranged by Ruth — Vickie asked "Is this Asian dance only, or will there be European groups also?"

"Nina has contacted someone in Leningrad, to discuss the possibility of bringing a group from the Kirov" Annisa replied "and a couple of other companies are interested -- an Australian classical company, another from Manila, and of course, one or two of the smaller US groups."

"Will there be a *wayang* performance?" asked Vickie "I've never been to one, and I have heard so much about the shadow puppets."

"Yes — there will! The most famous *dalang*—puppet master— in Bali has agreed to give one as part of the festival — be prepared to stay up all night. He won't start till midnight and then he'll go till dawn" Annisa said, laughing "we loved *wayang* when we were kids! The thrill of staying up till dawn, napping in a pile on the ground like kittens, the drama of the stories, and the ghosts and spirits of the night that we scared ourselves with!"

Her voice dropped to a quiet murmur ... "Bali is a ghost-haunted place where strange things happen, and where the gods and spirits are close to the people. It's been called The Island of the Gods; culturally it's a blending of Hindu, Muslim and animist beliefs with a sprinkling of Javanese court customs, and all overlaid by the playful Balinese spirit."

"The thing we noticed the most there" said Helke "was the music. It was everywhere. It was in the air wherever we went and also, everyone's an artist— musician, dancer, painter, sculptor, basket maker, maker of palm leaf decorations. Art truly permeates the air!"

Mark asked "Annisa, do you think that there will be more tourists after the new airport opens? And what do you think will happen to Bali then? Will it be changed?"

"I hope not but probably yes; Bali has always had visitors — artists, writers, musicians. Many of them came in the twenties and thirties to live here for a while and soak up the culture but distance and expense limited their numbers. We've survived a lot of invasions though, so tourists might not be so terrible. Their money though could be destructive."

"Well, I think it's time to go." Annisa folded her fan and stood up. "Ruth, Mark, this has been a delightful evening. I will be in touch soon." Ruth accompanied her to the door, where she said "Ruth, I think you are being watched— have you sensed it? I know I am always followed now, because Nina's husband and the KGB know that I am her friend and they are looking for information on her activities. While Paul was living, they left her alone, but now they think she's up to something. Be careful, and don't be too trusting! The watcher could be someone who seems to be in your camp!"

At a loss, Ruth stared at her. "Annisa, you are the second person in Jakarta to tell me to be careful and not to be too trusting! And no, I haven't sensed a watcher—I'll try to be more aware. Do I seem really naive, or is this such a treacherous place?"

Annisa touched Ruth's cheek with an affectionate gesture. "*Ma chêre* Ruth, you are as transparent as fresh water! Perhaps you need to cultivate a little guile! And, an old lady's advice — watch out for Vickie! She is neither kind nor truthful! *Bonsoir, ma petite — soit de bon courage!*" They kissed in the French manner, air kisses to each cheek, and Annisa, shivering slightly in the night air, pulled her silk shawl around her shoulders as she left.

Helke and Howard made their farewells also, and then George and Vickie. As they receded down the walk in the flickering light of the oil lamps, Ruth noticed George's hand now firmly placed on Vickie's shapely bottom, with no evident objection from its owner. A message to me, wondered Ruth, or just a target of opportunity? The pang of disappointment, maybe even envy, surprised her.

Bernie and Mark remained in the garden for a while, savoring their cognac and cigarettes; Ruth sat down to join them, and again felt Bernie's pain at the loss of his wife in such a horrible way. How terrible to be betrayed so completely by someone you loved, loved and trusted enough to bring two children into the world with her. "Whatever we can do, Bernie, let us know" said Mark as he accompanied him to the door, where the oil lamps were guttering out in the garden and the night dew fell thick as mist.

When Mark returned from the door, he found Ruth still in her chair in the garden, cigarette in hand. "I would like a cognac too, please" she said and waited quietly as he poured for both of them into the fragile glass bubbles from

Florence, then asked "So, to return your question of last week — how far has it gone with Vickie?"

Sighing as if to keep his patience, Mark replied "There is nothing to go anywhere between Vickie and me! I like her as a person, we had fun in Sumatra, end of story."

"You and Miss Texas looked pretty comfortable together down at your end of the table tonight! All snuggled together and giggling like kids. And you may not be interested ... yet, but she's working on you, I can see it."

"Well, ditto for you and Stewart! Please let's stop, Ruth, before we break something between us that we can't repair. Let it go! This chair's big enough for two — come and sit with me and enjoy the night. The moon is coming up."

They sat close in the chair as the garden filled with the warm moonlight of the equatorial night. Not the cool silver of the moonlight of the temperate world but, filtered through dust, smoke and humidity, gold light thick as cream poured over the shadows of the garden. Suddenly, Zoe bounded onto the grass in front of them, her head tucked down with her chin against her neck to conceal something large in her mouth. The patch of moonlight spotlighted her and threw her gigantic shadow on the lawn. Dropping the object from her mouth, she jumped back, stopped to study the creature on the ground, then skittered forward again to dab at it and force it to move. A large moth, it was alive, moving its wings and apparently unhurt. Zoe stood guard over it, quivering with tension and energy, then tried again to pick it up in her mouth. Ruth though intervened. "No, Zoe. Leave it!" she cried, and the little cat ran into the darkness.

As she gently picked up the moth and placed it in the mango tree, Ruth thought again of Zoe as predator — sleek, graceful, fast and merciless. Like many of the diplomats in Ruth's present world, she was attractive to the eye, charming, with a polished smooth elegance, but an efficient predator responsive only to her own wants. She thought of George Stewart, or Nina's husband, and perhaps also Vickie Ormond. But Mark's not like that--he's gentle, kind and cares for others. He doesn't subscribe to the old foreign service maxim-- "Nice guys finish last." He's right about us — we must let the grudges go and remember what he and I have — it is worth saving.

"Come back and sit with me, Ruth!" Mark called. She turned to him and pulled out the pins holding up the regal chignon she had worn all evening, letting her hair fall down around her shoulders, saying "I think we would be more comfortable in bed."

Mark laughed, and said "I've been wondering all night whether you are wearing anything under that disgraceful dress, but that hairdo made you seem so proud and unapproachable that I didn't dare ask. Will you tell me now?"

It was Ruth's turn to laugh, as she slipped the straps of the dress off her shoulders and let it fall to the grass "Does this answer your question?"

Chapter Twenty-six

Unravelling

Helke was restless as they waited in the conference room; diving into the enormous bag she carried, she pulled out a colorful mass of yarn: "I'm glad I brought my knitting. It's Saturday, so it's really a day off, and why are we here? I hate waiting."

"What are you knitting?"

"Busy work. Blanket for the leper hospital. Gotta show I'm a good little team member. And why did we have to come down here so early, and on Saturday morning too? Did I say I hate waiting? And ..." lowering her voice a little "I really don't like George Stewart! He's a snake!"

"Well, I agree, but what makes you say that now?" said Ruth, laughing a little at her friend's indignation.

"Didn't you see the way he was pawing Vickie in your garden the other night?"

"Well, I don't think she was objecting much!" Ruth answered, with a mental picture of George's hand on Vickie's *derriere* as the two of them departed her house, when the door opened and George Stewart entered the room.

"Good morning, ladies. I'm sorry -- I interrupted you, Ruth" he said. "Go ahead, I don't want to cut you off."

"Nothing important, we were just talking about knitting. Helke thought her piece was stretching too much." said Ruth hastily.

Ruth and Helke had been called to the embassy early on Saturday morning, and had not been told why. "Mr. Johnson, the *Chargé*, will be joining us in a moment, he's on the way. We are interested in your account of your lunch with Nina Smirnova and Annisa and want to hear it in person from you both. In the meantime, that was a lovely evening the other night, Ruth" George said "Great food, good company!"

"Glad you enjoyed it! Mark and I enjoyed it too. And I liked meeting Vickie after hearing so much about her. She's not quite what I expected."

"Some time I hope you'll tell me what you were expecting, Ruth. Be interesting to know."

Helke snickered. "Oops, dropped a stitch!"

The door to the conference room opened to admit a short dark-haired man, slightly plump, red-faced, sweaty and wearing tennis whites — Eric Johnson, *Chargé d'Affaires ad interim*. In the absence of the ambassador (almost permanent absence, thought Ruth, he hasn't been here more than a week since Mark and I arrived), Johnson was responsible for the affairs of the United States in Indonesia, including the welfare of its citizens and all visa and citizenship matters.

"Sorry to keep you — my Saturday tennis lesson with BamBam started late and I didn't have time to change. Gotta play early or it's too hot!" Greeting Helke casually with a smile "Helke, hi! You and Howard winning the duplicate bridge prize again?" then turning to Ruth "and you must be Ruth Fairchild. Good to meet you at last. I've heard a lot from Mark about you and your troubles with the Indonesian military police invading your home! And the problems with your former cook! All well now?"

"Thank you! Yes, we are fine, and pretty well settled in now."

"Well, let's get down to why we asked you both to come. Stewart tells me that you two have a story to tell that may throw some light on Paul Faber's disappearance?"

"We think we may have. Where would you like us to begin?" asked Ruth.

"Well, George has briefed me on everything up to your lunch at Taman Indah at Bogor, so could you start with that?"

"Alright. After I met Nina Smirnova by chance in the nursery garden, she gave my driver a note telling me that she is watched, but that she wanted to see me again and would be in touch. A few days later her friend Annisa called me and set up the lunch at Taman Indah."

"Why did you ask Helke to join you at the lunch? No offence, Helke — just a question. She wasn't with you when you met Nina, was she?"

"No, but Helke had seen Nina and Paul Faber together, and I thought she could be helpful. I relayed her information to Nina and she agreed that she should be there."

Helke, looking up from her knitting, said "As Ruth told you, I had seen Paul and Nina in his garden but I didn't know who she was. But when Ruth and I saw her at a dance performance at *Hotel des Indes*, Ruth recognized her and told me."

Ruth continued "When we settled at the table, Nina told us that she wanted to be in the dance world again and that she planned to leave her husband and defect from the USSR to America.

"Did she say why?" asked Johnson.

"Not right then, but later during lunch it came out. Security people from Moscow, KGB presumably, arrived at the embassy and ordered her to get to know a certain diplomat from the US Embassy and seduce him, with the intent to compromise him into giving information to the Soviet government."

Johnson and Stewart were silent but betrayed no reaction. Then Stewart said "Did she tell her husband about this?"

Helke, said "Yes, she did. This part really upset me, because it seemed so cruel and deliberately hurtful." She laid down the colorful piece of knitting she was working on "It's hard for me to imagine anyone acting this way toward their partner. He told her she had been naive to think that her privileged life came at no cost, and that now she was expected to pay. In her own words, '*I was to be the bait in a 'honey trap'. In other words, I was to be a spy. And a prostitute.*'"

Neither man said anything, and the room was again silent for a couple of minutes, until Johnson said "Did she identify the diplomat?"

"Paul Faber", Ruth replied for Helke, "my husband's predecessor. She said that a meeting was arranged somehow, and that she and Paul met at a dance performance at the Cultural Centre in Jakarta. Not to dwell too much on this — they met, they fell in love, and Nina confessed to him that it was a trap. She was afraid that he would denounce her and that she would be pulled back to Moscow in disgrace, but he didn't. Apparently as deeply in love as she, they continued to make plans for a life together. According to her, he planned to leave the foreign service and take her with him to the US, but... he never came back from a trip to the beach."

George Stewart spoke "Some of this we know. Ruth, you know this part too. After he disappeared, we had to pack his effects and notify his family. We learned that he had sent a will to his sister in Chicago, in which he left his large fortune to Nina Petrovna Smirnova — something that apparently dismayed his family--very conservative North Shore Chicago parents and sister, not thrilled at the idea of welcoming a Russian performing artist into their clan!"

"Howard and I witnessed that will! We didn't of course know what it said, but Paul came over one day and asked us to be witnesses to his signature" Helke said, and continued "Paul and Nina were being watched, you know", obviously surprising to both men. "My house overlooks Paul's garden. The garden is really quite private except from one upstairs window of my house, but along the fence line I found a place where the bushes and plants had been crushed and trampled, but I never saw anyone coming and going there. His driver, Suleiman, was often around other parts of the grounds though."

"Wait a minute, Helke" from Stewart "Suleiman, the same guy who was found dead in the embassy pool, wearing an expensive watch?"

"Are there other Suleimans in this story?" asked Helke tartly, a bit irritated at his tone "He was Paul's driver, and he was usually the one who brought Nina to the house. And I didn't know about the watch — Paul had a really nice watch that he said was a gift from his father when he passed the foreign service exams. Could that be the one Suleiman was wearing?"

"Would you be able to identify it as Paul's?"

"Maybe, I'm not sure."

Eric Johnson cut in "perhaps we can come back to the watch later. Ruth, tell me, how do you think that Paul's involvement with Nina Smirnova is connected with his disappearance, as you indicated to Stewart?"

Ruth, feeling challenged by Johnson's attitude, said "Well, first, I asked Nina what she thought about it, and she said she was 'full of suspicion', but that now he's gone and it looks like he'll never come back, she intends to continue alone with their plans for the future."

Helke had been nodding agreement with Ruth and said "After Nina confessed her role in the entrapment plot, he must have realized that he had to tell the embassy about it. This was a hostile attempt at recruitment of a senior US diplomat, and if it came out that he had concealed it, things would go badly for him and would certainly affect Nina as well."

"I was told that Paul had asked for a meeting with the top staff at the embassy" said Ruth "At least, that was the rumor. Perhaps you can confirm it. But it couldn't be scheduled quickly because of the ambassador's absence, and Paul went on the trip to Samudra Beach, from which he didn't return. So, the question seems to be -- coincidence? Or foul play?"

"Hmm. Interesting hypothesis" said Johnson "Stewart, thoughts? Can you confirm that a meeting was requested?"

"Confidentially -- yes. Security's already discussed the possibility of foul play, and although it would have been possible, I guess, how could it ever be proved absent a body?" George rubbed his head as if trying to massage some ideas out of it. "And how did Suleiman get Paul's beautiful watch? Also, when? And — who was the watcher in your garden, Helke? Why was he watching?"

Ruth felt it was time to raise something else, a question that had been floating in her mind since the night before, when Annisa had asked her if she were aware that she might be being watched. "George, how did you happen to arrive at Taman Indah just as we were having lunch with Nina and Annisa that day?"

"What? Oh - hm ... I think it was a half day at work for the embassy, and Gwen Edwards called up a bunch of people at the very last minute and suggested we make an excursion to Bogor for lunch — I think the Forrests were in the group, Vickie too, Gwen and her husband, maybe someone else, I'm not sure. Why?"

"It just seems odd. She called Mark at the office that morning when she couldn't get me at home, asking where I was. Mark said I was going to Bogor for lunch, next thing there she was with a little group for 'a last-minute outing'."

"Nina certainly wasn't pleased when she saw the group enter the restaurant!" offered Helke "I saw her face change color, and then she and Annisa made a fast exit. Something about that group scared her a whole lot!"

Chapter Twenty-seven

Nina Runs Away

The voices from the front gate floated in the window. Outside the fence, the thick darkness of the night was broken by bright hand-held lanterns that provided the main illumination. Without streetlights, the lanterns and the glow of flashlights made mysterious pools of bright and dark. Chatter and laughter, cigarette smoke, a small crowd gathering, shouts of "where are you going", answered by "to see the ice people dancing." The little crowd waiting at the gate included all of Ruth and Mark's servants and some members of their families. Bound for a performance of "Cinderella on Ice" at the sports stadium, tickets bought by Mark and Ruth as a reward for the household, excitement about this rare night-out was high.

Mark would take as many as would fit in the car, and bring them home at the close of the performance; Sunardi had gone to the market to fetch *betjaks*, the ubiquitous bicycle rickshaws, for everyone else. "Mark, how long do you think it will take you to drop them and come back?" asked Ruth.

"I don't know -- maybe forty-five minutes, if there's much traffic. Maybe I should just wait there in a cafe. Would you be alright if I do that? Anyway, come out to the gate and see this: everyone is dressed up, looking great."

"I'm coming! And I'll be fine here. I have letters to write and bills to pay." Ruth followed him out to the gate to see the theatergoers in their finery. The men wore clean white trousers and short-sleeved batik shirts, brown sandals on their feet in place of the ubiquitous thonged rubber sandals called "go-aheads" because if you backed up, they would come off your feet. The women wore their elegant traditional batik *kain*, ankle-length skirts tied sarong fashion at the waist and held in place with cummerbunds of bright silk, with long-sleeved lace blouses on top. Their long hair, smoothed with coconut oil, was wrapped into low chignons at the back of the neck and decorated with sprigs of jasmine from the garden.

Sunardi arrived with a small fleet of *betjaks*, and the party was away down the street. Mark waved as he set off with his group, and Ruth went inside.

The house, empty of all but Ruth and Zoe, seemed eerily silent. Normally a place of calm order, pleasant and welcoming now that it was furnished with their own familiar things, tonight Ruth felt it had returned to the cool impersonality she had felt when they first arrived. But of course, she thought, without Mark and the lively chatter from the kitchen and the back courtyard, it's pretty quiet in here. She closed the curtains at the windows and checked that all the doors to the outside were locked, put a record on the stereo, and settled at her desk to catch up on bill paying and correspondence. Zoe seemed reluctant to leave her, trying to get onto her lap and when Ruth refused to allow it, settling for sitting close to her on the desk where she could block most work from proceeding.

All seemed peaceful. Even the street appeared quieter than usual. Ramadan had ended recently, and Ruth thought people might be staying at home, tired after the long month of fasting and prayer. Suddenly, there was a loud clang from the street and the lights went out. The transformer again, thought Ruth, sighing as she recollected how long it had taken the last time to get the electricity *tukang* to ride his bicycle out to check that it needed repair. Lucky that Mark made me put a flashlight in my desk!

As she rummaged around to find the flashlight, she heard soft footsteps crunching slightly on the gravel of the path in the back courtyard She froze but didn't turn on the light because she felt safer in the darkness. There were fumbling sounds as someone tried to open the back door. KKkkkkkk from a gecko startled her, made her jump. She felt the cold shadow of fear. From where she sat, she could see the door, a thin line of light at the bottom, probably from a flashlight, interrupted sometimes by a shadow when the person outside moved. He tried the door, but it was firmly locked, and she saw the light disappear as he moved away, presumably to try to gain entry elsewhere. She knew that in order to get to the phone -- which might or might not work, depending on the mood of the *hantu*-- she needed to cross the room in the dark, avoiding sofas, chairs, and miscellaneous furniture. She decided to wait and not risk revealing her presence by showing a light.

Again, there were the soft fumbling sounds, this time from the door to the garden, with the thin line of light showing at the bottom of the heavy wood door, and the shadow of movement outside. Her desk was close to that door, and she could hear heavy breathing. Then the key turned in the lock and the door slowly began to open. He has a key! Panicked, her heart a rapid drumbeat, she tried to move away and as she did, she tripped over Zoe, who gave a loud wail of insulted feline protest. Alarmed, the intruder fled noisily away from the door towards the street where there was a little light from the faraway street lights. Ruth quickly pulled back the curtain and caught a glimpse of a man dressed in European clothes, and looking very much like Joe Forrest.

Joe Forrest! What on earth? As she stood at the window still looking out into the darkness and looking for meaning in this, she saw a shadow move in the garden, and she could make out a slight figure approaching the open windows of the living room. She drew back, nervously trying to conceal herself. The figure came closer and knocked quietly on the window, saying softly "Ruth! Ruth! It's Nina -- are you there? I need help!"

For a moment Ruth thought -- I was just planning to pay the bills tonight. What next?

"Nina! What are you doing here? Are you alright?" she said through the open window. "Just a minute till I find the flashlight -- I must have dropped it when I fell over Zoe."

With the flashlight, she could see Nina outside, apparently trying to conceal herself in the bushes, and ran to bring her in the garden door. Nina said "Quick! Hide me some place where no-one outside can see me!" and Ruth, stung by the urgency and panic in her voice, half-pushed her into the bedroom where the windows were frosted glass and the curtains drawn. "I ran away from the residence, and it was lucky that the lights were out when I got here so no-one could see me come into the garden."

"But, how did you get here? I didn't hear a car."

"I took a *betjak*. No-one would expect to see the ambassador's wife in one!" Nina said, laughing a little hysterically. "I never rode in one before."

"Sit down, Nina" Ruth said, indicating the end of the bed "I will make a cup of tea, unless you would like something else. And then you can tell me what this is all about."

"Tea would be wonderful. And yes, I will explain as best I can."

Ruth fetched candles, and heated water for tea on the kerosene stove in the kitchen. When she returned to the bedroom carrying two glasses of strong sweet tea, Nina was still sitting on the bed, crying quietly. She didn't look as well-groomed as usual: her dress was wrinkled, a sleeve was a little torn, and her long hair was straggling out of its usual tight knot.

"Thank you for taking me in, Ruth. Perhaps you would call Annisa for me. Your house is closer to the residence than hers, so I came here. She will arrange for someone to pick me up and get me safely to her house. I won't go back to my husband's house."

"Nina, what has happened? What should I tell Annisa?"

"Just tell her that I was asked to do something I cannot and will not do. She will understand, and she'll shelter me until I can get away from Jakarta."

Annisa answered the phone quickly, and said she would have someone come to the house for Nina. Ruth suggested that she could be picked up at the next-door house which had a driveway accessible from the side of the Fairchilds' garden not visible from the front gate; Annisa agreed, and said that a *betjak* would come for Nina.

Back in the bedroom, Ruth told Nina the plans. "Can you tell me what has happened, Nina? Why did you leave in such distress, and why can't you return? And why does Annisa feel that so much secrecy is necessary to get you out of here?"

"Ruth, I am in terrible danger. I can't tell you why. But I must warn you that you and your husband are involved. Please be careful."

Ruth, still puzzling over Joe Forrest's attempt to gain entry to their house, said "Nina, please tell me what it is, so that we know how to protect ourselves! A man tried to break into this house just before you showed up. You may both have been in the garden at the same time. He looked like Joe Forrest, a staff member ...." Nina interrupted her.

"I know who he is. He was at Bogor when we had lunch together and he is why Annisa and I left so hastily. I have seen him at our embassy, talking to the KGB men. I don't know what he wants."

"Nina, what happened tonight to make you run away? Can you tell me, so that we can try to figure this out and get more help for you?"

" I was told to seduce your husband and compromise him. I refused and I was threatened with a beating. As soon as I got a chance, I slipped out and came here. They will be looking for me."

Ruth sat down hard on the edge of the bed. I wish we were back in Paris, she thought.

Chapter Twenty-eight

The Debriefing

Around midnight, Mark's car and the returning *betjak* fleet rounded the corner near the cigarette kiosk under the flamboyant tree, passengers quiet, sleepily murmuring to one another about what they had seen and heard: a foreign fairy story, "Cinderella", not just acted but skated on ice. They recognized the wicked stepmother, the ugly sisters, the good and beautiful heroine, all understood by Indonesians who lived with the stories of the gods and goddesses of ancient India and Java and their amazing adventures.

Music! Dancers swooping and twirling, shockingly bare-legged women in scanty costumes, jumping and spinning, to music like none the audience had ever heard before. Lights! Like the shadow plays — shadows turning and stretching, crossing, twisting, sequins and jeweled costumes flashing in the darkness, moving to the rhythms of the music, with skates hissing and spraying cold water from the ice. Ice! And such ice! Not like the cubes made from boiled water that came out of Ñoña's refrigerator, but a great white sheet, smooth, hard, and large enough for people to dance and whirl and spin! Astounding!

Sunardi paid the *betjak* drivers, while everyone else stood around for a few minutes stretching and yawning in the late-night dewfall, smoking last cigarettes, until someone noticed the lack of lights in the neighborhood.

Ruth, after seeing Nina to the *betjak* sent by Annisa, had returned to the house and waited nervously for Mark's return. She heard the group arrive, but waited till people dispersed before running out. "Oh, Mark! I am so glad you are back! The lights went out and I was so scared and I fell over Zoe and she may be hurt ... and I hardly know where to begin! Oh, it's just been awful, a man who looked like Joe Forrest tried to get in, and Nina was crying in the bedroom and ..."

Mark said "Honey, I'm sorry you were frightened! " With his arm around her he walked her into the house and asked "How long have the lights been out? Let's get some more light in here, those two candles aren't much use. I'll find the lanterns."

Calling out to Muriarti in the kitchen, he asked " 'Ti, please bring some tea for Ñoña and see if you can find the lanterns! Ruth, honey, calm down! Just sit here quietly with me, take some deep breaths, and then you can tell me what happened" Ruth, usually so self-possessed and confident, had broken down completely. The events of the evening had been cumulative -- the fear of the intentions of the prowler outside, the shock of Nina's appearance, and then her incredible revelation -- all had combined to undermine her poise and assurance.

Producing a big white handkerchief, he dabbed softly at her face, saying "there, there, don't worry. I'm here, everything's going to be alright. " This produced more tears, but gradually she calmed and could begin to organize her thoughts.

Muriarti brought tea for Ruth and a kerosene lantern, its soft light illuminating only the area immediately around their chairs, giving her a feeling of intimacy and safety.

"Ruth, could you try to begin at the beginning -- what was the first thing that happened?"

"The first thing was when the lights went out and I heard someone moving around stealthily in the back courtyard..." As she related the story to Mark, he was quiet, letting her tell it at her own pace.

When she had finished, he said "Wow! A member of my own staff tries to get into our house, using a key that he has somehow obtained? And I am the target of a Soviet intelligence-gathering operation? What on God's green earth is going on here?"

"Now that it's over and you're here, I can think a bit more clearly." said Ruth. "First question I have, apart from what he wanted, is —did Joe think that there would be no-one in the house tonight?"

"Maybe he heard about my ticket purchase, and assumed that we were going to the show with the group. I got the tickets through the embassy admin office; I think I told Vickie that we were treating the staff, but I didn't say much else. She asked her secretary to get the tickets and bring them to me. Joe must have thought it would be a good opportunity to snoop around--for whatever his reasons were--and was shocked when he realized that someone was home. "

"I can't think why he would do such a thing!" Ruth sighed "Second question, then, where did he get a key?"

Mark said "Ruth, we really need to know what he was doing and why, AND we need to figure out a way to proceed. We can't just go from one of these incidents to another without finding out what is really going on. But -- I don't know who to trust now!"

"Don't you think we can trust George Stewart?"

"I suppose we have to. I'm going to call him now. I don't care if it is after midnight, he can get over here and help us!"

A call to George, with a brief explanation of what had happened, produced him a few minutes later and with him, Vickie Ormond, both looking sleepy and slightly disheveled. "I live just the other side of Blok M" he said "and I thought we might need Vickie's admin experience too, so I picked her up on the way."

"Ah, Stewart" said Mark "glad you could get here. Vickie, good to see you. We really need some help. Ruth has just had a very frightening evening; I'm going to ask you to tell the story again, Ruth, if you would."

"I hope I can help" Vickie said sweetly. Sleek blonde Vickie, a cat full of canaries and cream, claimed vaguely to have come directly from a dull evening alone at home. Ruth doubted it: her slightly imperfect appearance -- hair a little tousled, messy makeup, wrinkled trousers and blouse -- gave Ruth other ideas. The air between George and

Vickie almost crackled with sexual tension, expressed in voice, gesture and glance. She is so open about their affair, Ruth thought, I think she's up to something. But what? An affair with George is not unusual around here, he tries it with everyone, so it can't be that! Annisa's warning to her about Vickie came to mind -- she's neither truthful nor kind. I wish she weren't here.

Ruth said quietly "Yes. I'll go through it again. I'm calmer now, so I may remember some things I didn't recall when I told Mark about it."

She told the story again, but this time George stopped her with questions. "How long after Mark and everyone left did the lights go out, Ruth?"

"I'm not sure" she replied "I was busy getting settled, checking doors -- maybe half an hour."

"And how long after that did you hear the prowler at the back door?"

"Again, not sure, but only a few minutes, I think. Do you think he could have managed to shut down the transformer somehow?"

"I don't think it's possible without special tools and knowledge" replied George "More likely, it was a surprise -- a gift from the gods. I'm sure he appreciated it! How long was he at the back door?"

"A few minutes. Then I thought he had gone, but he reappeared at the garden door. I suppose he didn't know which door the key fitted. Oh! I think I remember now about the key!" Ruth interrupted herself "Mark, remember when Joe Forrest met us at the airport the day we arrived? He did this eager-beaver real estate agent act, showing us around the house. When he left, he gave us the keys, but said there was one missing and he would check on it? Maybe he kept the garden door key deliberately."

She continued-- her fear, falling over Zoe, then seeing the man fleeing and recognizing him as Joe Forrest. George stopped her then "How sure are you of that, Ruth? There wasn't much light and you only had seconds to see him."

"About 90%. It was fairly obvious he wasn't Indonesian -- he was big, kind of bulky; and he was wearing American-type clothing--beige trousers, a dark short-sleeved shirt. He was bald too, like Joe."

"Do you have anything of special value in the house?" asked George.

"A couple of pieces of art, Grandma's silver tray, Mark's record collection -- stuff like that. Nothing of enormous value, nor anything easy to sell quickly."

"Was he carrying anything when you saw him?"

"I don't think so, but it was such a quick glimpse…"

"It's possible he had something he wanted to leave here. Papers, plans, drugs, stolen goods -- something illegal, perhaps with the idea of compromising one or both of you. Thanks, Ruth."

"Wait" she said. "You haven't heard the rest of it" and continued, quickly recounting Nina's dramatic arrival and departure, and her revelation about the planned honey trap being set for Mark. When she had finished, she drew a long breath and said "There. That's all I've got."

"Let's get more light in here! There should be a couple more lanterns in the *godown*, and Muriarti will bring tea if anyone would like it" Mark offered, then called to Muriarti in the kitchen.

Siti and Muriarti arrived a few minutes later, still wearing their festive finery, carrying a tray of tea and two bright lanterns. Placing the tray on the coffee table and the lanterns around the room, Muriarti reached into the cummerbund at her waist and pulled out a tiny notebook. In her halting English, she said to Ruth "I ... found at back. Is yours?"

All eyes in the room focused on the little book. Ruth took it from her with a word of thanks and began to examine it: black leather, with the year 1968 in gold letters on its cover, it was the kind that many men carry to remind them of appointments; there was no name on it, but there were numerous entries in tiny script next to certain dates: "R -- cafe w/G?" and "M/V work late" were recent entries. Hmm, looks like we all have something to be embarrassed about here, thought Ruth.

"The prowler must have dropped it" George reached over and snatched it from Ruth's hand. Let's have a look at it." Rifling through the pages, he said "Goes back about a year. It's all hard to read though. Mostly just initials and sometimes what looks like Cyrillic! Anybody here read Russian?"

Exasperated, Mark said "Stewart, you're the embassy security officer. You must know that Ruth and I both speak some Russian! Why pretend you don't know that? But it might not be Russian -- lots of other languages use the Cyrillic alphabet. Give me the book, please. Ruth, let's look at it together under one of the bright lanterns."

Crossing the room, Ruth picked up a large magnifying glass from her embroidery table in the corner and returned to her seat next to Mark, where, using the magnifier, they began to look carefully at the tiny volume. Entries appeared to go back to the beginning of the year, mostly just initials but occasionally a brief notation such as "Check this" or "why?"

"There's not much Cyrillic" Ruth remarked "Just a couple of past dates have it, but there aren't many entries for future dates anyway." Flipping through pages quickly, she stopped at one and said "This is about the only pending thing -- it's about three weeks from now, and it just says 'HC' -- I wonder if that's a person or maybe a place?"

There was silence in the room. Then Vickie said "Well. I reckon we arrived at the OK Corral just in time for the gunfight."

Chapter Twenty-nine

More Visitors

"It's good to see you, Gwen! I'm glad you could come for coffee" Ruth said as they met at the door a couple of days later. "Come and sit in the garden. We need to catch up! I've missed you -- were you on vacation?"

"Yes, we took a shopping trip to Singapore." Gwen answered as they settled into chairs in the shade. Ruth thought that with her pink and purple Pucci-print dress, and her sharp-eyed glance, more than ever she resembled an exotic bird come down from the mango tree to roost in the garden chair. "Anything exciting going on here?"

"Not really, although Mark's in Singapore right now for a day or so to see the dentist. We had a little dinner party last week, and that was interesting. Vickie Ormond came, George Stewart, a couple of others. Tell me -- what do you think of Vickie?" Ruth, fishing blatantly, tried to look innocent.

"Oh, Vickie! My, how that Texas charm is slathered on! She is certainly making a play for George--not the first to do so, mind you, but he just might be in danger this time. She's got a reputation for efficiency!"

"But I thought George is married, wife back in the States -- not true?"

"Well, I heard a rumor recently that she is in process of divorcing him. I guess if she had wanted to keep him, she would have come with him. Might not have worked anyway -- he is a terrible womanizer. But you already know that." Gwen chuckled, and Ruth realized that her friend was teasing her with a reference to her lunch with George. "Actually, I think Vickie is a bit jealous of you -- she suspects that you were flirting with him, so she decided to put a stop to that."

"Wow! He had better watch out or she'll have him at the altar! As for my flirting with him, really Gwen!" Feeling herself on dangerous ground, Ruth quickly changed the subject: "Have you seen the Forrests recently? What are they up to?"

Gwen settled back happily, readying herself for a juicy gossip session. "Well, they have been pretty quiet. Joe had a fall apparently--turned his ankle somehow the other night, and now he's using a crutch."

"Too bad. How did he do that?" asked Ruth, wondering if his rapid exit over their gate could have had anything to do with it.

"I'm not sure." Gwen accepted the cup of coffee offered by Siti, and returned to the topic "Belinda said he was out for a walk one evening a couple of days ago and fell down. Had to come home in a *betjak*, in the dark."

Ruth reflected on the avidity of Gwen's interest -- she seems overly stimulated and excited by gossip. I've noticed it before, she thought, and it's unpleasant. Useful sometimes though, and to be encouraged right now.

"Why on earth would anyone go for a walk in the dark around here? Walking is hard enough when you can see the broken sidewalks and the trash." Ruth remarked. "Did she say why?"

Gwen took cream and lots of sugar, and continued "Didn't say, but being Joe, he probably saw some important person going by and wanted to impress him. You know, those two are completely driven -- Belinda wants to have a finger in every pie, to be Mrs. Senior Wife, to run everything, and Joe -- he wants to be ambassador. Not to do the hard work, but to be Mr. Big, swan around meeting-and-greeting, living the good life and meeting important people."

Siti appeared with a plate of cookies and put it on the table next to Gwen, who took a deep breath and two cookies and launched into further details of Joe's ambitions. "I think he expected to be made economic counselor when Paul disappeared -- he has the necessary seniority, but not the professional experience. I hear tell he isn't an economist, just pretends to be one."

So -- Joe thought he would replace Paul Faber as economic counselor, even though he isn't an economist, thought Ruth. Wants to be an ambassador, and Belinda would like to play Mrs. Ambassador too. But the powers-that-be picked Mark to be the new economic counselor -- Mark, an actual experienced economist with qualifications. Must have caused some heartburn in the Forrest household.

"Do the Forrests have any special friends here? Anyone they spend time with -- play tennis, bridge? I mean -- what do they do for fun? They can't work all the time."

Gwen said "Well, Belinda is just so bossy that she puts people off, and Joe is a bit heavy--no sense of humor, wants to talk about his career prospects, how to get ahead faster." She hesitated for a moment, but it was too tempting to add a little gossipy speculation: "They seem to be quite wealthy, have more money than the average foreign service couple. Big expensive car, and their house is much larger than anyone else's--did you notice that when you went there for dinner? I think they must pay more than the rental allowance. They have a lot of art -- pretty good, I think -- not the standard tourist stuff. They do a lot of expensive entertaining, too."

" Well, the food was good the night we were there. Who do they invite?"

"Oh, other diplomats, Indonesian bankers and ministry officials, World Bank and IMF people. Some US embassy people too, for the mix."

" Would they invite people from the Soviet embassy?"

"Not very likely. We don't have the best relations with the USSR right now because of Vietnam. I can't imagine why they would be included." Gwen stopped, and looked at Ruth "Remember when Solange told us about seeing Paul in the restaurant with Nina Smirnova? I've wondered ever since how they met and what kind of relationship they had. It just seems so unlikely that the two of them would be having an affair, doesn't it, but from what Solange said, there doesn't seem to be much doubt about it?"

"I suppose not. Nina is gorgeous! And really nice too -- I can see why someone would fall for her." And, hoping to encourage Gwen a little "Do you think her husband knows?"

"Of course he does! If he doesn't, he's the only person in Jakarta in the dark! That day we saw you up at Bogor -- we were all talking about it after we saw her leave in such a hurry, and wondering how you and Helke knew her." Well, Ruth thought, that answers the question of whether they saw Nina that day!

Casually, she said "Helke's dance connections got us an introduction. Nina is working on a dance festival to be held in Bali in a couple of months, and she is looking for sponsorship. She hoped the embassy might be a source."

Gwen, taking another cookie, said "Are you and Mark going to the festivities for the opening of the new jet airport in Bali? It's in a couple of weeks, and seems like everyone who's anyone will be there!"

"I hope so -- we just learned about it, and Mark's planning to get reservations."

Getting up from the chair, Gwen said "This has been lovely, but I must get going. Maybe see you at the pool later." They walked together to the door, then Gwen stopped and said "Oh, heavens! I forgot -- did you hear about the missing papers? With Mark away, you probably didn't hear. A bunch of classified memos and cables are missing from the embassy safe. Pretty inflammatory stuff if it got to the press apparently, according to my husband. It's a major security breakdown, just came to light late yesterday, and people are running around in circles trying to sort it out."

After Gwen left, Ruth decided that after dinner and a glass of wine, she would sit down quietly and think things over. The discovery of papers missing from the safe was disturbing, but hardly something she could do anything about; I'm sure Mark will be upset about it when he hears, but he probably won't hear till he gets back from Singapore. It's Thursday, so the servants will leave before dinner for their weekly day off, and won't be back till Friday night. Some music, comfortable robe and slippers, an early night, and careful thought about what Gwen had told her.

The house was quiet. With the lamps dimmed, Debussy on the stereo, another glass of wine at hand, Zoe curled into a relaxed croissant beside her and a feeling of peace and harmony filling the room, she relaxed. Joe with a sprained ankle! Wish he had broken it! Took a walk in the dark, did he? She felt herself drowsing off to sleep, put her feet up and stretched more comfortably on the sofa, careful not to disturb the sleeping feline, and let her thoughts roam free, soon falling sound asleep herself. In her dream, the hand stroking her breast through her robe felt good, she thought, warm and soothing; she felt her senses awaken, turned a little to allow the fingers to unbutton the robe, and smiled a little. She lay back, sleepy and satisfied with this pleasant dream, and opened her eyes to see George Stewart's face close to hers and felt his lips on her mouth. Damn, it's George! I really should object, I suppose, but is there any harm, really? She opened her lips and allowed his tongue to explore, as he continued to fondle her thighs. Oh, how pleasant! He really does know how to please one, she thought, no wonder he is so successful with women!

He turned to better position himself for his victory, and .... Yowl! Screech! Hiss, yowl, scream! The protests of an insulted feline were startlingly loud and close. "Damn this bloody cat!" roared George "Get it off me!" Zoe, blue eyes wild and hair on her back raised and staring, clung with all 16 claws to his back as he tried to shake her loose. "I didn't know it was there and I kneeled on it! Get rid of it, and come back here!"

Ruth, no longer drowsy and dreaming, stood with a heavy glass vase raised in two hands, poised to bring it down on him. "That was attempted rape!" she shouted. "Zoe, get off him. Thanks, little one!" Zoe released her grip and ran out of the room, while Ruth continued to menace him with the vase.

"You weren't objecting, dear girl" responded George "In fact, I thought you were having a good time. Certainly sounded like it -- mmmmmm, ohhhh, ahhhhh." Ruth gestured threateningly with the vase and he said "Oh, alright" and began to put his clothes to rights, chuckling a little as he did so, saying "I knew you would like it, if you would just relax and not be so starchy. But never mind. Nothing ventured, nothing gained."

"Get out" yelled Ruth. "Don't touch me again, don't talk to me unless in an official situation with a witness present, and don't flatter yourself that I want to have an affair with you."

"Ruth, I don't need to rape a woman to get her into bed with me. I'm never that short of willing candidates! And don't YOU flatter yourself either -- you were an interesting challenge. I'm not interested now that I know how easy you are!"

"OutOutOut! Now! And don't tell anyone, if you value your career. I won't tell Mark because I don't want him to ruin his career by attacking you. For the sake of appearances, I will continue to treat you as a respected member of the embassy community, but do not touch me again nor talk to me alone. Ever." Then, she thought of something -- "How did you get in here? All the doors are locked. I checked them myself."

Moving to the door, out of range of the heavy vase, he grinned and said "Embassy has a master key. I got it out of the safe this morning." as he disappeared out the door into the darkness.

Chapter Thirty

Meeting between Mark, Ruth, George and Helke

"So ... we're back at Cafe Sarinah" Mark said "doesn't look any more inviting this time than it did before. George has got to stop meeting us like this."

Ruth thought I would rather he would stop meeting us at all, but I can't say anything about that. She made a murmur of agreement; Mark was right about the cafe. The floor was stickier than before, and the smell of *trassi* -- the concentrated fish paste used to flavor some local dishes -- was very strong. "Well, Helke said she's included in the meeting this time, so that's good. And there she is, coming down the arcade. Look, she's got her knitting bag on her shoulder!"

Vivacious Helke, dark short hair curling around her face, brought a spring freshness with her. Almost smells like lilacs in here, Ruth thought, it's that New England background of hers. White churches on the village green, "Little Women" and ivy-covered campuses, bread-baking mothers, fir trees, long knitted scarves with fringes, and winter cold -- practical and good in an unassuming way. "Helke!" Ruth called out "I am so glad George included you this time! We need your Maine common sense here in equatorial Asia!"

Helke laughed as she heard this. "Well, we're definitely living a tourist's dream in this cafe! I wonder when it was last cleaned." She sat down in the chair next to Ruth and rummaged in her big bag, producing a clean blue dust rag and a little bottle of Lysol, saying "Let me clean off the table, at least. Do you think George doesn't know any other place to meet -- this is disgusting! There are lovely places upstairs. Why does he insist on meeting here?" as she scrubbed the table carefully.

Mark sneezed as the Lysol smell hit his nose, saying "Perhaps because it is so dirty that no-one we know would come here and we won't be recognized. Maybe there's method in the madness." Ruth wondered what else the knitting bag might contain in its capacious depths. Who is Helke? Why is she always so prepared? Is she an actor in this tangle, or just an innocent bystander?

"When did you get back from Singapore, Mark?" Helke asked.

"Last night. Came back just in time to find everyone running round in ever-expanding circles, looking for the stuff that disappeared from the safe. George is up to his eyeballs in the search."

George sloped into view, still wearing his daytime office suit, but stripping off the tie and unbuttoning his shirt collar as he approached the table. "Careful, George" Helke said "don't go too far with the strip tease. Ruth and I are delicate flowers."

"Very funny, Helke" he said grumpily "not in the mood today. No sign of that classified material yet. Could be really embarrassing to the US government if it gets to the press! Anybody want coffee?"

No-one responded and Ruth asked "George, is Joe Forrest involved in the search?"

"Yes, of course. The cables concerned a delicate negotiation which went through the embassy's economic section quite recently. Mark handled it, pretty soon after you got here."

Mark nodded agreement, and said "it seemed pretty routine at the time, although yes -- not something to spread in public. I can't say any more about it, but it is worrying that this stuff is missing."

"Have you entertained the possibility that Joe took the papers? And that he planned to plant them in our house the other night, to get Mark into trouble?" asked Ruth "If it's so sensitive, Mark could be charged with a major security violation, couldn't he? I don't know about here, but in Moscow that would be a reason for removal from post, and maybe firing from the foreign service."

"Yes. We have considered that scenario. Can't say any more now" replied George "Helke, you are probably wondering why you are included in this gathering."

Helke, who had been knitting quietly, laughed and said "Oh, nothing about Jakarta surprises me now but I am a bit curious. So, do tell me."

"We would like you and Ruth to go to Bali a couple of days in advance of the opening celebrations for the new airport, to meet with Nina and Annisa and help set up Nina's defection. Then, when Vickie and I get there along with everyone else, things can be put into motion quickly."

Thrifty New Englander Helke said "who's paying? Howard and I are planning to go for the celebrations, but we don't want to pay for extra hotel nights. Will I get per diem?"

"All taken care of, Helke, and Ruth too. You will be Annisa's guests at her family home up in the mountains -- should be interesting!" George grinned "Traditional Balinese hospitality -- lots of people, interesting food, music, dance, up all night watching shadow puppets. You'll love it!"

Ruth, also like Helke taken by surprise, asked "What do we have to do? And when do we leave?"

"Next week. Work with Annisa and her contacts. She is using her family and friends because she and Nina feel that they are more trustworthy than officials in the Indonesian or US governments. We will make some money available for you, to pay for tickets or other necessities, and you will be carrying Nina's Soviet passport -- she got it to us right after she left her husband. Bernie has already issued her a US visitor's visa. I know I don't need to tell you to keep it quiet!"

Ruth was silent for a few minutes before saying "Mark, did you know about this? And Helke's husband -- did he know too?"

He answered "Yes. Sorry I couldn't tell you before now. This is important, and we are trusting you and Helke to pull off some difficult stuff that we can't do ourselves."

"We've been sidelined, Helke! They think this busy work will make us feel useful!" Ruth exclaimed. Mark and George had allied together to plan for Nina's defection, throwing her and Helke the bone of "helping Annisa". Getting the women out of the way, more likely. I suppose I will have to go along with it right now, but I won't be so willing to share information with them in future. As for our marriage -- it's definitely sustaining a blow today. Not that George looks much more appealing either!

Helke, red-faced, angry and sputtering, pulled her chair nearer to Ruth so that they were close, a firm feminine wall. No longer the charmingly vivacious young wife with the amusing eccentricities of the enormous handbag and the knitting, she stood up -- five feet of righteous indignation, holding her ground and scolding imperiously. "Just what do you rulers of the universe think you are doing? Moving Ruth and me around as if we are pawns on your chessboard. Diplomats, huh? Big brave men making big plans, and you don't even know that there's a mole in the embassy?" She stopped for breath, glaring at the men.

"Helke, we know that." George broke into her tirade. "It explains a lot of things that have been happening. But right now, we have to take action without tipping our hand to the Soviets. We need you and Ruth to take care of Nina while we deal with the mole, and then get Nina safely out of Indonesia and on her way to the US."

Ruth, patience gone at last, shouted "You must know that Joe Forrest is the mole, so why are you waiting to arrest him? Nina saw him talking to the KGB at the embassy! She told me that the other night when she came to me for help, and Mark -- I told you that and I am sure I told you too, George. And now he's trying to compromise Mark with stolen papers. What more do you need?"

"Proof, Ruth" Mark said quietly. "The papers weren't put in our house. We don't know where they are. Maybe they are already with the KGB, in the safe in their embassy. Maybe he found someone in the old town who paid him for them, intending to cause a scandal for the United States. We don't know, and we need proof. Joe is being followed. In the meantime, please go to Bali and help us get Nina out."

George added "If you two go to Ubud to stay with Annisa, it will look like planning for the dance festival. And a social event as well. We aren't trying to shut you out! Just asking you to do something you are both good at!"

"There's just one more thing, guys" Ruth stood up, leaving Helke still seated "What about the notebook? Why is there a notation "HC" on the day of the opening of the international airport? That's the only future date in that book -- everything else is in the past. What's going to happen that day, apart from the new airport? And what does "HC" mean?"

"Those are my initials" said Nina as she walked into the café. "HC" is "NS" -- Nina Smirnova, written in Cyrillic. Sorry I'm late. I was followed, and I had trouble getting a *betjak.*"

Chapter Thirty-one

Helke Takes Control

The Garuda plane turned to a southeastern course as it crossed Bali Strait, the slender strip of water between Java and Bali, and in the distance, Ruth could see the conical shape of *Gunung Agung*, the highest volcano in Bali, its shoulders wreathed in clouds and emitting wisps of smoke from its crater. Beside her, Helke knitted; the peaceful clicking of her needles had accompanied their journey. From her knitting bag, she had produced provisions from time to time -- juice, cheese, crackers, fruit, and a small bottle of wine for them to share.

"Helke, you are a positive traveling PX! What else do you have in there?" asked Ruth.

"Well, ask me for something, Ruth. Test me."

"Eye shadow."

"What color? I have mauve, green, blue, silver... Really, Ruth, that's too easy! You can do better than that! Try again."

"Alright, if you insist. Ummm -- a gun."

Helke rummaged in the depths and produced a tiny pearl-handled pistol, a "lady's gun." "Don't worry" she said, seeing Ruth's look of alarm "I know how to use it, although I've never fired it except for practice."

"Put it away, Helke! Quick, before somebody sees it! It's probably illegal to show a gun on an aircraft, even one that looks like a toy!"

"Well, I guess you're right", she said, putting the minute firearm back in her bag. "When Howard joined the foreign service, my mother was afraid I might find myself in danger some time, so she bought it for me and sent me for shooting lessons. Only time I've thought about using it was when I found a cobra in the house in India, but I was afraid I would miss and disembowel the sofa or something."

"What did you do? About the snake, I mean."

"Oh, I yelled for the cook and he chased it out with the broom. Look, we're coming down."

As the plane landed, they could see the new glass and steel terminal in the distance, with a few planes snuggled up to it. A military plane was undergoing maintenance out on the field, and there was no indication that a major celebration would take place in a few days. They exited the aircraft directly into the air-conditioned terminal, and Ruth remembered her arrival in Jakarta only a few months before -- out of the plane into the hot steamy air, walking across the baking tarmac to the shabby building, the confusion inside, the crowds of people coming and going. Tourists will like this much better, she thought.

Helke said "Look, there's Annisa over by that fountain", and they made their way toward Annisa and the little group of people surrounding her. She greeted them warmly with air kisses, and smilingly introduced her companions.

"This is my brother, Gusti, and his wife Dewi" she said as she presented a handsome middle-aged couple. Gusti shook hands with them in the European manner; Dewi smiled shyly but didn't offer her hand. "And this is my son Nyoman--who is also our driver" continued Annisa, adding as they shook hands "he knows all the highways and byways of Bali, and is looking forward to showing you around the island. So -- let's go!"

The car, a large gray Mercedes, waited outside the main door with the engine running and a boy leaning against it, presumably keeping guard. Nyoman gave the boy a small bank note, and Annisa ushered everyone into the air-conditioned car, saying "we'll be comfortable in this car today, but tomorrow Nyoman will take you both out in the jeep. It's much better for touring because it can tackle some of the mountain roads where this one would be useless!

"Nina is already here. She is staying in the old house with us--we thought it would be safer than a hotel for her, and for you also." said Annisa, as the car glided quietly down the palm-fringed road.

"Gusti and Dewi know about Nina's problems, and we can all talk freely. Our home is a little outside Ubud, and everyone in the household is carefully watching for strangers in the area. Next week there will be a lot of tourists, with the opening of the airport."

Nyoman opened the sliding glass window between the front and back seats, to point out the scene they were passing in the village. "See the big bamboo cages? Those are the villagers' fighting cocks--they are put out by the road during the day, so that they can be entertained by watching the people and cars passing. These birds are treated like royalty!"

Dewi chimed in "Yes, until they lose a fight. Then, they're dinner."

Suddenly, the car accelerated and swung fast into a narrow path which led off into the bush. Nyoman said quietly "We're being followed. I thought so when we left the airport. Annisa, I'll take the back way, the path the women use for the temple festival preparations."

Annisa assented, saying to Ruth and Helke "it won't be the most comfortable ride, but the Mercedes can do it. Hold on!" The car swayed and billowed, its soft suspension stressed by the rough path but Nyoman continued to drive fast, with Gusti peering out the back window for the sight of any following car.

"No one in sight" he reported. "We might have lost them. Will this car ford the stream up ahead like the jeep would?"

"No idea" replied Nyoman "but we have to try! Let's hope there're no *karabao* wallowing around in the water!" As he spoke, the car nosed through a wall of tangled foliage across the path, and a rocky stream appeared. It was not very wide and appeared shallow, but running fast over and around large rocks. The big car slowed as it entered the water, then sedately and with great dignity crossed the turbulent water without apparent effort and emerged onto the opposite bank without damage. The passengers congratulated Nyoman, who said modestly "All in a day's journey in Bali! We'll be back on the main road in about a kilometer, and it's pretty smooth from now on."

Annisa said "Well, I am relieved that we apparently lost our followers. We've cut our journey by about 10 kilometers by taking this path, and they probably won't be able to figure out where we were heading anyway because there are several branch roads up ahead. I suppose it's Nina's husband and his KGB helpers."

After some precautions to be sure they were no longer being followed, they proceeded on the narrow main road for about fifteen minutes more. Ruth was nervous that they would be followed again, but all was calm and at last the car pulled up at two carved stone pillars, surmounted by a roof of palm fiber, with a white-painted stucco wall stretching to each side. Gusti said "We're here." and they exited the car, Ruth still a little jittery but Helke apparently completely confident. Well, she's got a gun in her bag, thought Ruth. They walked between the pillars to find a wall facing them, obliging them to turn to the right or left in order to enter the compound. Gusti laughed, and said "The wall is to confuse the evil spirits. Apparently, they can't turn corners very well--no guarantees that it works on Russians though."

As they left the car, Nyoman said "I will take the car around to the back gate -- this is an old traditional house and there's no place in the compound for a car. I will see you inside in a few minutes and we can talk about this problem."

Inside the stucco wall of the compound, the floor was of beaten earth, clean swept, with a large and striking frangipani tree in the center and flowering bushes and vines around the perimeter. There were no sounds but the noise of the wind in the surrounding bamboos and soft Balinese voices. As they entered, a woman walked toward them from one of the small buildings that dotted the space. Moving with lithe grace, she wore a batik *kain*, a simple cotton blouse, and rubber sandals; her oiled black hair hung loose down her back, with a frangipani flower tucked into it. Suddenly, Ruth recognized her -- "It's Nina! Good heavens, Nina! Look at you -- you look marvelous, so relaxed, and so different!"

Nina giggled. "Marvelous what a vacation can do! And borrowed clothes! Annisa's been working on me -- oiling my hair, helping me tan a little, painting my toenails! You like the new Nina?"

Laughing at Nina's nonsense, Annisa said "we thought a disguise would be a good idea, and I loved turning Nina into a Balinese beauty! I think it would be hard to be sure this was Nina if you didn't hear her speak." Gesturing to Nina, she said "Nina, could you show Ruth and Helke to their room, please? Then, we will meet in the *balé* for lunch and a little planning. We need to discuss what just happened."

Nina showed Ruth and Helke to a small square building with a heavily thatched roof; two steps led to a porch floored with polished wood beneath the roof. The thatch was supported by carved wooden pillars, and there were no walls or doors, only moveable screens and curtains.

Inside were two small sleeping spaces with mosquito nets draped above the beds, each curtained off from the other, and a simple bathroom. The sleeping rooms led to a little balcony at the rear, looking into a wildly-tangled private garden of banana trees, flowers and vegetables flourishing next to the inner side wall of the compound. Ruth sighed "It's magical! We'll just get settled and freshen up, then will you show us the way to the ... *balé*, Nina?"

"Yes. The *balé* is the biggest of the pavilions, and it's where everyone gathers. You can see it - towards the back wall." Nina pointed to an elaborately thatched building, its roof held up by carved wooden posts, with some low chairs and benches scattered on the polished stone floor. It formed a single large room, cooled by wind and protected from rain and sun by the overhanging eaves.

The ladies settled their belongings and, refreshed, joined Nina to walk toward the *balé*, when the dreamlike silence was broken by rough shouts, loud male voices from the back of the compound, and the sound of running feet. Ruth pushed Nina roughly back into their pavilion forcing her into the enclosed sleeping area. Helke stood on the steps outside, groping in her knitting bag, and shouting "Get out! Leave us alone! We're Americans!" Then, producing her tiny gun, she pointed it in the air, and fired.

To Ruth, it seemed like such a small sound, hardly a gunshot at all. But its effect was astonishing. The intruders -- two men in European clothes -- froze in place, then quickly recovering their powers of locomotion, sped toward the front gate. The spirit screen baffled them temporarily, and Helke fired again into the air. They vanished around the screen, with the members of Annisa's household pursuing them enthusiastically.

"Well! That was ... fun" said Helke, as she slipped the gun back into her bag.

Chapter Thirty-two

A Traditional Balinese House

The group that met in the *balé* an hour later was subdued, frightened by what had just happened, and definitely uncertain of how to proceed.

"Somebody knew that Nina was here and wanted to grab her" Ruth said "how did they know that? Only Mark, George and Vickie should have known. Not even Helke and I knew till Annisa told us in the car."

"Nina, could someone have seen you at the airport or on the plane?" Helke asked.

Nina said "Oh, we drove. Nyoman and his friend brought Annisa and me from Jakarta in the friend's car. It's about a thousand kilometers, but we decided it would be better than taking a plane. We stopped for a night in Surabaya then drove to Ketapang and took the ferry. We left the borrowed car there, and picked up Annisa's grey car on the Bali side of the strait. I don't think we could have been followed. Do you agree, Annisa?"

"I think it would have been difficult. There are long stretches of road in Java where there is no traffic except ox carts and local buses and any tail would have been easy to see."

Ruth, still grappling with the problem of how Nina's whereabouts were disclosed, asked "How did you get away from Jakarta, Annisa? And did you notify George that you were leaving?"

"I told the servants in Jakarta that we were going to spend a couple of days in Jogjakarta, making some plans for the dance festival in Bali. Then we left very early the next morning in the car with Nyoman, but for Bali not Jogja," then, pausing for a moment, Annisa continued "and I tried to phone George but he wasn't available so I spoke to Vickie, telling her we were leaving."

"Do the locals know where your house is located in Bali? And would many people recognize your gray Mercedes?"

"Oh, anyone could find out where my house is -- just ask someone. Bali's essentially a big village. And a lot of people know the car -- there aren't a lot of luxury European cars in Bali, given the state of the roads."

"So" Helke tried to summarize "so far, it's possible you got away from Jakarta without detection. The most likely place for someone to have picked up your trail may have been at the ferry dock in Gilimani, when the Mercedes showed up to get you."

"Looks like it" Ruth said "whoever it is probably recognized Nina and followed you here, then back to the airport to pick up Helke and me" and turning to Nyoman "it was clever of you to spot them on the way back, but they already knew where we were going, I guess. But it's puzzling -- why did they wait until today to try to kidnap Nina when she's been here for a few days now?"

Annisa stood up. "We need to phone George or Mark. Our phone here is very old fashioned, and if we want to make a long-distance call, we have to go to the Bali Beach Hotel in Sanur. They have some kind of fancy phone service. Ruth, will you come to the hotel with me so that we can make the call? It's an hour earlier in Jakarta, so we should be able to reach them at the embassy."

With Annisa driving, the big gray car slipped quietly down the mountain road till it reached the coastal plain, with sandy beaches and coconut palms bordering the road. Lined with brilliant tropical flowers and bushes, the driveway into the hotel wound through an extensive park before reaching the doors of the hotel. Annisa said "I'll go and talk to the manager, to see if we can use the hotel's phone lines. He's Swiss, and very helpful."

She continued "We have rooms booked here for everyone -- you, Helke, Nina, me, as well as the Jakarta group. Best though if we stay at my house till the last minute, and till George and Mark get here. Why don't you come in to the lobby with me, while I find M. Monfils?"

Annisa leading, they left the car and entered the lobby, where a crowd of staff and visitors milled about. Frivolously, Ruth thought I wish I could wear my clothes with as much glamor as Annisa! She's so tiny but has so much dignity, and she makes a simple *kain* and *kebaya* look high-fashion; the high-heeled gold sandals she wears with them are elegant; I don't know how she manages to drive a car in them, and to walk so regally though. I feel utterly plain when I'm with her.

"Oh -- there he is! M. Monfils, it's Annisa! Could you help us, please? We need to contact Jakarta urgently -- would it be possible to use your phone line for a few minutes.?"

"*Mais bien sûr*, Madame Annisa -- for you, all is possible!" M. Monfils showed them into a small office with a table, two chairs, and a telephone. "Dial 9 to exit the hotel switchboard, then just dial the Jakarta number" he said as he left the room. "If you need help, ask the reception desk."

Ruth reached the embassy switchboard and was quickly connected to Mark "Oh, Mark! I am so glad to hear your voice" she said. "So much has happened since Helke and I left this morning, and I am so worried. Annisa and Nina are here, safe at the moment--did you know that? But I don't think we should all stay in Annisa's house after this. Where are George and Vickie, and is there any chance that you could get down here quickly?"

"Not right now, Ruth, but I think George and I can get there tomorrow as planned. I am happy that Nina and Annisa have turned up -- one less problem to solve! The embassy is in even more chaos than usual! Joe has disappeared. He left his house sometime through the night, leaving everything behind except what would fit in a suitcase, apparently."

"What? How ... What on earth is going on?" Ruth cried, then turned to Annisa to tell her this news and then asked "Is Belinda alright?"

"She's still here, completely confused and bewildered. Looks as if she didn't know what Joe was up to. I don't know what she's going to do."

Annisa said " Do they know where Vickie is?"

"No, I don't know where she is at present. She was here last night" Mark said, having heard Annisa's question "George is at the Forrest's house now, trying to find any information that might indicate where Joe went, and why. We are checking the airport and the sea port also."

"Oh, and Ruth -- remember the initials 'HC' in that little book? They were written against tomorrow's date, and it looks as if something big is planned for tomorrow, so be extra careful."

"And what should we do now? Evidently Nina isn't safe at Annisa's house" fretted Ruth "Would it be safer if she came here to the hotel?" Then she realized that it was possible the telephone line was bugged and, using "Arabella", an old warning from Moscow days, said "By the way, Mark -- my friend Arabella's in Indonesia now too. She'll want to know about all this."

"Interesting!" said Mark "She's possibly heard already. Anyway, George and I will be there tomorrow, in time for the *wayang* performance at the hotel."

"I'm worried about Arabella, Mark. She's very unpredictable. I don't think I will say any more on the phone until I am sure what she knows." With that, she hung up and, turning to Annisa, said "Let's go, Annisa. I think we should all move to the hotel today, Nina too. Mark and George put Helke and me in this position and now it looks like we're in charge. Let's go home and get packing."

As they left the hotel, Annisa caught Ruth's arm, "Look over there. Isn't that Vickie? Over by the *barong* at the other side of the lobby -- she doesn't look like she did at your house though. See? Next to the *barong,* the big lion mask?"

And yes, Ruth realized, it was Vickie, almost unrecognizable, no longer the impeccably dressed and sophisticated foreign service officer but a most unsuitably dressed tourist -- very short shorts, blouse with no sleeves, cut low in front and partly unbuttoned even lower, bare midriff, lots of makeup, and gaudy clattering bangles and necklaces. Her companion, an older man sweating heavily despite the aggressive air-conditioning of the lobby, had his arm around her shoulders as she spoke to him in a braying Texas accent "Would you look at this thang? Is that some kind of bad dream?" Could it be ... Oh, no, Ruth -- you are hallucinating. Is it though? Yes, she decided. It IS Joe Forrest.

Chapter Thirty-three

Ketjak Dance

The reception hall of the Bali Beach Hotel was crowded when Ruth came down from her room; tourists and politicians and staff milled around the high-ceilinged space in a bewildering blur of bright colors, excited chatter, and music from the gamelan in the corner; a constant stream of new arrivals entered from the gardens outside the doors. Ruth and Annisa had arrived from Annisa's house a couple of hours earlier with Helke and Nina, and checked into their reserved rooms. There was no sign of Vickie or Joe, and Ruth was still considering something that Nina had said in the car, when she and Annisa had described Vickie's appearance at the hotel with Joe Forrest.

"It was so strange!" Ruth had said in the car on the way from Annisa's house to the hotel. "We had just learned that Joe had disappeared, presumably defected, and was being sought frantically. And there he was, in the airport in Bali with Vickie. I wanted to go back and call Mark in Jakarta again to tell him but there wasn't time because we needed to get us all safely to the hotel, and when I tried to call from my room just now there was no answer from the embassy or my house. The phones get worse every day!"

"Yes" Annisa had added "and this was not the Vickie we knew in Jakarta, but a bizarrely-dressed young woman ... What on earth was she playing at?"

"Maybe she wanted you to notice her" Nina had put in "could she have been sending you a message? Perhaps there were watchers around and she didn't want you to get caught up in something."

"Oh!" Ruth said "Yes -- she wanted to draw our attention to something -- Joe, maybe. That could be it! She was a caricature of a tourist-- tight revealing clothes, dyed red hair, a lot of cheap jewelry, and loud ignorant comments about Indonesian cultural objects. I thought she was showing off, and she didn't seem to recognize us."

Was Nina right that Vickie was warning them, reflected Ruth now. But if so, of what? And what was she doing with Joe Forrest, the allegedly fleeing US official? Whose side is she on, wondered Ruth.

Annisa and Nina, who were sharing a room, arrived with Helke close behind. "We'll have something light to eat now" said Annisa "then we can have dinner later, after the Ketjak dance." As she led them out of the hotel doors into the space between the hotel and the sea, Ruth saw a swimming pool glowing a deep-ocean blue on the edge of the beach. Small tables covered in cloths in intense colors -- purple, deep green, azure blue, brilliant yellow, printed with gold Balinese designs of flowers and leaves --were placed beneath the palm trees surrounding the pool, with the white sand and pale blue of the sea beyond. Barefoot waiters in white uniforms and gold cotton headdresses were moving around serving guests from a lavish buffet.

As they seated themselves, Ruth saw what she now recognized as the split column of a stage entrance a little distance away, and Helke said "That's the Ketjak Dance space. It's an amazing spectacle -- I think there are more than 100 dancers in the Sanur club, and quite a lot of drummers as well."

"We have reserved seats" Annisa said "but it won't start until dark, so let's get some food and then claim our seats."

They placed their orders with one of the waiters. "What do we know about the Ketjak dance" said Helke "I have heard of it but don't really know anything but its name."

As their meal arrived, Nina said "It's quite impressive. I saw it once when a troupe visited Jakarta. It's not really old, but it is taken from a story in the Ramayana. A German artist, Walter Spies, lived in Bali in the thirties and he developed the dance as a tourist attraction. It's loosely based on a Balinese trance ritual, synchronized hand waving and chanting -- "chakachakachakachaka", faster and faster, until it all blends into an indecipherable mass of sound. It's striking, and I am hoping it can be included in the dance festival here."

"Time to get our seats, ladies", Annisa said as they finished their meal. They walked toward the split column which marked the stage entrance of a semi-circular outdoor performance space. In the center of the stage stood a tall bronze lamp with four fiery arms radiating from its trunk; torches were placed at the rear of the stage, providing the only illumination as the sea darkened and the tropical night came. Tall bleachers faced the stage, and Annisa, after asking the attendant about their seats, came back to say that they could not all sit together and would need to split up into two groups. "Some kind of muddle about reservations, I suppose. It happens all the time in Bali!"

Ruth, concerned about Nina's safety, went to try to convince the attendant that they needed to sit together but with no luck. "Did you bring your little gun, Helke?" she asked, and when Helke assented, said "That will at least be some protection. Could you sit with Nina then, and Annisa and I will sit together?" Then, after a moment, she added "And stay in your seats at the end until Annisa and I come and get you"

The great oil lamp and the torches lit the performance space with smoky flickering light, while the sound of the waves from the beach carried clearly to the assembled audience, until the low muttering of drums overlaid it, indicating the beginning of the dance. Across the space Ruth could see Nina and Helke in their seats against the side of the bleachers, and felt reassured that there was no way that anyone could get to them except by disturbing the seated spectators. Movement on the stage distracted her, and she turned her attention to the dance.

Two men appeared through the split columns, each carrying a large black and white checked parasol which they placed carefully, flanking the entrance. The men withdrew, to allow a horde of men to enter. Naked to the waist, they wore short skirt-like trousers, checkered black and white like the parasols, red sashes around their waists and flowers behind their ears. They poured onto the stage and formed concentric circles around the large oil lamp, holding their arms up in synchronized gestures, and chanting "chakachakachaka" as they knelt and continued their stylized gesturing and rhythmic movements.

Dancers appeared from time to time in more familiar dance costumes, representing characters from the Ramayana -- Rama himself, Sita his wife, kidnapped and held to ransom by Ravanna the evil giant, Hanuman the monkey king -- the chanting dancers represented his monkey army, sent by him to help Rama rescue Sita.

To Ruth, the setting and performance were stunning -- the hypnotic chanting, the light from the smoky torches and the oil lamps, the ambient glow from the nearby sea, and as the light of the sun faded completely, the brilliant stars above it all. Without the light pollution of cities, the Milky Way blazed across the sky, the Magellanic Clouds strikingly visible from this latitude. The performance lasted for an hour; as the performers left the stage and the torches began to dim, Ruth realized she was exhausted by the intensity of the experience on top of the anxiety of the past days. She and Annisa sat silently for a moment or two before looking around for Nina and Helke, only to see empty seats where they had been sitting. "Annisa, they've gone!" she cried, as she pushed through the departing crowd toward the place where she had last seen them. "They're not there! What happened? How could they get out of here without us knowing?"

They began to ask some of the people who had been sitting in the area if they had noticed anything during the performance. A British man said he thought Nina and Helke had been sitting right in front of them "I noticed them because they are both so pretty" the man said, as his wife rolled her eyes at him. "I think someone handed something up to the dark-haired one from below -- she was sitting at the end of the row. I heard her cry out, and I shushed her, because she was disturbing my concentration, then they got up and pushed their way down about five rows to get out. That's all I know."

Ruth asked if they could remember any words, and he said "Well, it was hard to hear because of the drumming and the chanting, but it sounded like "He's here! Poll's here!"

Chapter Thirty-four

Nina and Helke Disappear

Ruth and Annisa stared at one another in shock. "Paul's here?" But Paul -- Paul is missing, presumed dead, gone for almost six months now. How could he suddenly turn up and in Bali of all places? And where are Nina and Helke? And what do we do now, Ruth thought.

"We need to report this to the police," said Annisa. "Hurry up, Ruth --let's get into the hotel and get to a phone."

"I don't think we should do that yet. We don't know for sure that anything bad has happened. If Nina got a message from Paul, she would be so excited that she would just run off to meet him, and probably Helke would go with her to be sure she's alright. Maybe we'll hear from them soon."

The crowd was dispersing quickly, many walking toward the rear entrance of the hotel. "Yes, let's get to a phone, Annisa-- I want to try to let Mark and George know what's happened."

As they entered the hotel foyer, they saw Mark and George standing at the reception desk. "We were able to get here a bit earlier than we expected but there's only one room available. Ruth, can I share a room with you?" asked Mark "It's been a while since we ... umm... shared. My option's to share with George ...."

"Doesn't appeal to me much either" said George grouchily. "I'd rather share with Ruth than you."

"Cut it out, George--no time right now to reopen that! Mark, I am so happy to see you. We're not feeling very strong and independent right now," Ruth replied, and she and Annisa, both talking at once, started to pour out their fears and worries--the story of Nina and Helke's disappearance, of the sighting of Vickie and Joe, and of Vickie's strange behavior.

"Wait! Slow down, you two! We can't understand anything you're telling us." ordered George. "Sounds like you're saying that you saw Vickie here today and Joe and Nina dyed their hair red and ran off together!"

"Reopen what?" asked Mark, catching up. "I didn't know there was ever anything that needed to be closed. Has there been something between you and George, Ruth?"

"Only in George's mind" snapped Ruth. "George, get this straight, now and forever. There is nothing doing between us. Go back to Vickie, she's the one who dyed her hair red. Joe doesn't have enough hair to accept any hair dye." Her voice rising angrily, she said "Now, can we get down to work? Nina and Helke have vanished, Joe is here in Bali, Vickie looks like a strumpet and is hanging onto Joe like she's madly in love with him, and I wish I'd never left Illinois."

Annisa said softly "Let's find a quiet place to sit so that we can discuss this. We are making a scene, and people are staring. Come along, everyone" shepherding them toward the back of the lobby like a bunch of mutinous sheep, and calling to M. Monfils for help. He guided them discreetly into a secluded rear lounge, and left, with a muttered

"*Bonne chance!*" to Annisa. Thanks, Ruth thought. We're gonna need good luck.

They settled sulkily in their chairs. No-one spoke for a few minutes. Then George said "Ruth, you have a spider on your blouse! Hold still ..."

"Keep your hands to yourself, you lecher! Hold still, Ruth -- I'll do it!" As Mark moved toward her, Ruth put up her hand and flicked the insect onto the floor. Mark, a bullfighter delivering the *coup de grace,* crushed it with his foot, then sat down and, with a deep sigh of satisfaction, said "So ... what's next?"

"Truce?" said George. "I will if you will."

"Truce" replied Mark "for now."

Nyoman rushed into the room, saying urgently "I've been looking everywhere for you, Annisa. What are you all doing back here? Are you hiding?" I saw Nina and Helke leave during the performance, and I know something's wrong!"

"Nyoman, you saw Nina and Helke leave?" asked Annisa, the first of them to comprehend the message. "How did you see them? Where? Tell us, quickly!"

Nyoman began to answer, but George stopped him with an imperious gesture -- "I am going to pull rank now. I am the embassy security officer and I will ask the questions." Nyoman looked surprised, but shrugged his shoulders and waited for George's questions.

"What did you see?" began George.

Under her breath, Ruth whispered "Oh, hurry up!"

"I was out in the car park during the performance, cleaning the car and talking to the other drivers. There were a lot of cars there, and a lot of strangers -- usually I know everyone, but tonight was different, I suppose because of the airport ceremonies and all the visitors. I was smoking with a couple of friends, when I noticed something going on at the dark end of the lot."

"What do you mean -- 'going on'?"

"Well, it was a bit dark to see properly down at the end, but I could make out two women being led to a van there, and they looked like Nina and Helke -- remember, I had seen them in our car a couple of times today? When someone inside the van opened the door, Nina looked in and said something I couldn't hear, then she grabbed Helke and tried to run away."

"What did Helke do?"

"She resisted Nina and started scrabbling in that big bag she carries, yelling something about Joe and a gun, but a big guy jumped out of the van and grabbed the bag away from her, then he and the man who had brought them to the van pushed Nina in, then pulled Helke in too. I guess there was another man inside who was the driver, and they took off fast."

"Could it have been an American who jumped out of the van?"

"Maybe. He was big, pale, no hair."

"Any identification on the van?"

"Yeah, it said 'Kuta Beach Shuttle'. Doesn't mean much -- anyone can put something on the side of a van, call themselves a shuttle. Tourists gotta watch out!"

After a few minutes of silence, George said "I think we need to enlist the local authorities. This has gone beyond my capacity of security officer. And I am worried about Vickie now, too."

"Vickie?" said Ruth disbelievingly "She's probably in the van with Joe, having the time of her life."

"Ruth, I know you resent Vickie, but I need to tell you -- she is a brave young woman. She's a CIA agent, has risked her life in Vietnam and Cambodia, and has been assigned here for a special purpose."

Mark said "The special purpose isn't administration, for sure! No wonder Eleanor was running a drug ring out of the admin office -- it's amateur hour. Security officer and CIA agent, neither of whom could administer a one-car funeral."

"Mark, please drop it!" Annisa said sharply "It isn't helping anything or anyone. You can take it up later if you still want to." Mark, grumbling under his breath, subsided and

Annisa continued "George, I know the officer in charge of the military detachment in Denpasar. His name is Colonel Suradji; I don't know the phone number but I'm sure the reception desk will know how to contact him."

Colonel Suradji and his lieutenant arrived a few minutes later, announced by the *pam-pom* of a siren and accompanied by a small detachment of smartly uniformed military police. "At your service, Madame Annisa" said the colonel as he shook the elegantly-manicured hand Annisa extended to him. She introduced George Stewart as the US Embassy's security officer, and Colonel Suradji listened intently as George related the events of the evening, stopping him only once or twice with questions, then saying "We have been concerned today with the arrival of an aircraft registered in the USSR. It had been due to arrive here two days ago but was delayed by weather on route from Moscow. It is supposedly an Aeroflot craft under charter, but we have not been shown a passenger manifest nor informed of what business it has in Bali. Its flight plan now calls for it to depart from Nguyen Raj at 11 o'clock tonight."

Annisa said "I am a friend of Madame Nina Smirnova. She and an American citizen, Mrs. Helke Ramsey, vanished from the *ketjak* performance tonight. We think that they have been abducted by Soviet agents who are acting on behalf of her husband, the Ambassador of the Soviet Union to Indonesia, who is also a KGB agent.

George spoke with firm authority "Madame Smirnova is a Soviet citizen, we believe that the plan is for her to be taken on board this chartered plane tonight for involuntary repatriation to the Soviet Union. She does not wish to return to that country.

"In the light of the forcible seizure of Madame Smirnova and her companion, Mrs. Ramsey, we request that the Indonesian government issue an order to prevent the aircraft from leaving Bali until further inquiries can be made." said George.

The colonel stood silent for a few minutes, maintaining his upright military posture while apparently reflecting on his options, then turned to his lieutenant and gave a sharp order: "Radio to airport to hold plane, don't permit refueling." Turning to the group, he said "we don't have much time. It's 10:30. We need to get to the airport now."

Chapter Thirty-five

Helke Returns

"Nyoman, run and get the car! We'll meet you at the front door. Colonel Suradji, we'll follow you, just give us a minute to get the car here." Annisa, tiny despite her 6-inch gold heels, beautiful and strong-willed, had slipped into her favorite roles: event controller and manager of people. Again, she herded her little flock, rapidly reaching the lobby and the front door, now less crowded and quieter than earlier in the evening. "Don't go away! Just stay here and wait for Nyoman!" she ordered as George began to show signs of straying.

A black limousine purred softly into the covered entryway, neatly blocking Nyoman and the gray car from reaching the door. As Annisa and her group watched with frustrated impatience, the uniformed chauffeur got out and opened the door for a passenger to alight. A gust of sandalwood perfume preceded the appearance of a tattered and unkempt Helke, saying as she emerged "Thank you so much, Your Highness! You rescued me and I am completely in your debt! Goodnight, and you must bring your wife to dinner with us in Jakarta."

Turning toward the entrance and seeing the flabbergasted faces of her friends, she said "Well! I'm certainly glad to see you all here waiting for me! Where's Nina? And has anyone seen my knitting bag?"

As the limousine pulled away, the gray car pulled up to the door at last and Annisa, still in her event controller persona, said "Helke, we are going to the airport. Get in the car and we can talk on the way." Helke nodded meekly and joined the others as they crowded into the car. Nyoman put the car into line behind Colonel Suradji's two jeeps, and the little column pulled out, accelerating rapidly on the dark road to the airport, sirens sounding as they went.

Ruth said "Helke, you first! Where's Nina, is Paul here, and where have you been?"

"I have been stranded on a rural road in Bali. Some Russians dragged Nina and me into the van, but they didn't want me, only Nina. I was put out of the van a couple of miles after we were grabbed in the parking lot. Paul wasn't in the van. The note to Nina saying he was waiting for her was a fake. The country people who saw me on the road thought I was the evil witch Rangda -- white face, wild hair, walking alone at night -- and wouldn't help me."

Annisa said "They were probably terrified! Rangda is seriously wicked! Who is the man who picked you up -- the one you called 'Your Highness'?"

"Oh, he's an Arabian prince, learning his royal job by being his country's ambassador to Indonesia. He picked me up on the road when no-one else would! His name's Khalid, and he's a delightful young man! He and Howard will really get on well, and he's going to bring his wife to dinner when …"

"Thank you, Helke", said George "can we save the social notes for later?" The car was traveling fast now, behind the military vehicles. The road was smooth but curving, and the passengers swayed back and forth with the motion. "Do you know who the people are who took you and Nina?" he continued.

"I think they're KGB; they were snarling at Nina in Russian and she seemed scared. Oh, I forgot. Joe Forrest was there, and he was speaking Russian too. I feel a bit carsick. The prince's car was impregnated with sandalwood! I wish I had my bag with my medication in it."

"And Paul--is he here? And did you see Vickie?"

"Well, the note said ... um ... 'I'm here at last! Come now, someone will meet you at the exit and bring you to me ... love, Paul.' But it wasn't true. A strange man met us at the exit but when we got to the van, Paul wasn't there, only the Russians and Joe Forrest. Joe took my bag and my gun! And no, no sign of Vickie."

"Thanks, Helke! Now, why don't you rest for a bit and Ruth will fill you in on what has been going on since you and Nina left." George turned to Ruth, and asked "Would you mind, Ruth? Mark and I need to make some notes, and plan a little strategy. Mark, how's your Russian these days?"

Mark answered "Not as good as it was, but I have kept it up a bit and I could certainly interpret if things don't get too heated."

Ruth nodded and confirmed this, saying "Mark has kept up a lot, using tapes and reading", and then said "Helke, we're on the way to the airport to try to intercept the KGB's plan to put Nina on a Soviet plane and return her to the USSR. The plane is supposed to take off at 11 o'clock, but Colonel Suradji, the officer in charge of the Bali detachment of the military police, has issued an order to prevent that from happening. We must be almost there, I think."

The screech of brakes and a sudden deceleration of the big car showed that Ruth was correct. The military jeeps had stopped and the policemen were taking positions at the doors to the terminal, apparently permitting no entry or exit for the general public.

Colonel Suradji said "The Russian party is being held in the transit lounge at Gate Number 4. The plane is at the gate, but the boarding ramp is not in position, and refueling has not taken place yet. We need to go to the gate where I can give permission for them to exit the lounge, on the pretext that they will be boarding immediately."

"Will we be able to ask Madame Smirnova if she is leaving willingly?" asked Mark, as they walked through the terminal toward Gate 4.

"No. This has become an international incident, and you are permitted only to observe. I represent the immigration policies of the Indonesian government in this matter. I will put the question to her."

Mark continued "Then, if she indicates that she does not want to return to the Soviet Union, what will happen?"

Suradji said "She will be taken into protective custody and a decision in her case will be made by a special court." He paused, then said "Here we are. This is Gate 4. The door at the rear of the space is the transit lounge where the group is being held."

Annisa cried out "Oh, no! Taken into custody? Can't she just come home with me and stay until she can leave for the US?"

"The court will act quickly. It is possible that a decision will be made tonight. So, let's go. The door will open in a second."

The wide doors to the transit lounge were behind a bank of escalators, and were difficult to see -- visibility from inside the lounge was probably not good, and the location may have been chosen for that reason. A tall screen stood to one side also, providing cover for several military police individuals who waited behind it.

The doors swung open and several Indonesian officials emerged, followed by three men in neat white shirts and dark trousers -- presumably the crew of the Aeroflot aircraft. They walked briskly toward the door leading to the plane, but were stopped by one of Suradji's men before they reached it; seeming confused, they talked together but then waited quietly for further orders.

Joe Forrest appeared at the door of the lounge, with Vickie holding onto his arm. When he saw the little group of Americans and Indonesians at the gate, he stopped and tried to return to the transit lounge, but was pushed to the side and thrown to the floor by Vickie and given no opportunity to warn the others in the Russian party. Vickie, still in her garish tourist outfit, quickly dragged him behind the screen, gagging him with a scarf from her hair, binding his wrists and ankles with several of her "necklaces", and immobilizing him by sitting firmly on him.

"What did I tell you?" muttered George. "That girl's got guts!"

"She's got a talent for accessorizing", murmured Helke to Ruth.

Chapter Thirty-six

Nina's Plea

Suddenly, three people were in the door of the transit lounge: two burly men holding a slender woman by the arms, supporting her as she slumped between them, one foot in a high-heeled black shoe, the other bare and hardly touching the floor. Nina.

Her head thrown back, and her right hand pressed to her heart, she appeared to be in emotional pain, with no trace of her usual light carriage. Her eyes were half closed, and the jacket of her tailored red suit, surprising garb in a tropical setting but probably appropriate for Moscow, was wrongly buttoned, giving her a disheveled appearance, strange for the carefully-groomed woman Ruth knew.

Grim-faced, the men holding her stopped abruptly as they encountered the scene outside the transit lounge. The short grey-haired man who had been following them pushed roughly past the group and said to Colonel Suradji: "Let us pass. I am Igor Smirnov, Ambassador of the USSR to Indonesia. My wife is in need of medical care for conditions caused by the climate in Indonesia and must return to Moscow immediately. Who are you and why are you blocking us?"

"I am Colonel Suradji, official representative of the government of Indonesia and I have reason to believe that this lady is being repatriated to the Soviet Union against her will."

Ambassador Smirnov, without customary diplomatic smoothness or tact and with his face reddening alarmingly, shouted angrily "You have no right to interfere with our passage! It is imperative that my wife receive medical treatment in Moscow as soon as possible. I demand that we be allowed to leave immediately."

Suradji gestured to his men to move closer to the party of Russians. "Madame Smirnova, are you returning to the USSR willingly, without force or coercion?"

Nina attempted to moisten her lips -- they seemed too dry to form words. She tried to free herself from the men holding her arms but without their support, she swayed a little, too weak to stand firmly. Facing her husband, she made a balletic gesture of rejection, holding out her hands with palms toward him and pushing firmly, symbolically distancing herself from him, then covered her face with her hands in an attempt to hide her tears.

"Madame Smirnova ... Nina ... we need to hear you tell us what you want" the colonel said. "I ask you again. Please reply clearly."

Smirnov angrily shouted something in Russian at Nina, and the colonel said "English only, please."

Nina seemed again to struggle with finding her voice, but at last she said softly "I do not want to go with my husband. I do not want to return to Moscow."

"Release her!" Suradji said to the two Russians holding her and, turning to the group "Annisa, please help her now." The men ignored him and continued to hold her arms.

Annisa began to move toward Nina, but Igor Smirnov shouted "No! She's a Soviet citizen! She is my wife and will do as I say." To the KGB agents holding her, he said "Continue taking her to the plane." One of the men hesitated, but the other pulled Nina roughly away and began to try to drag her toward the plane.

With great effort, Nina stood her ground. She shook her arms free and cried out "Igor, don't do this -- please! We loved one another once -- for what we were to one another then, for what could have been, please let me go!"

He walked closer to her, facing her "You must come back with me, Nina! You are risking my career, even my life, if you defect! Why aren't you loyal to me -- your husband? How can you do this to me?"

"Loyal?" Nina 's soft voice became shrill with anger "Loyal? Your loyalty was never to me, only to the KGB and your 'career'. You used me as a bargaining chip! '*See my wife? Pretty thing, isn't she? Tempting little morsel to bait a honey trap, don't you think? She was a ballerina, you know*' Isn't that how it went, Igor? Twice that I know of, you offered me as a sexual prize to obtain information for the KGB to use against its enemies, and you dare to mention loyalty to me?"

"I did it to get a better life for us! To get us out of the Soviet Union, to live better than we could in that country..."

Suddenly, he looked around nervously, realizing his mistake and perhaps wondering which of the Russians present was an informant and adding "and, of course, to help our country to move forward." Then, after a long minute, as if tired and accepting his defeat, he said quietly, without drama or emotion "I had no choice, Nina, no choice at all. Forgive me."

Ruth, among the silent watchers, felt pity for the man. Caught in a system which set its people against one another, he had played as well as he knew how, used the chance he had to make a tolerable life inside the organization, but ultimately been consumed and destroyed by it.

But now Nina had stepped outside his control, and was playing for her own chance at freedom, at a life outside Russia, a life where she could use her natural gifts and her training, and learn to trust herself and the people around her.

"Igor, I can't come back -- not to you nor to Russia. I still remember the affection we had for one another -- and I weep for its loss. I weep too for the loss of my country, my poor sad country. I forgive you. Please give me your permission to go now."

Smirnov hesitated for a moment, then stepped close to her and took her hands, holding them to his lips. "Nina, little Nina, you could always reach my heart if I let it open to you. When did it go wrong? How did we get to this? Go, little one. Dance Juliet once more, and remember me."

Turning to Colonel Suradji, he asked "May we leave now. My wife will stay here."

Suradji nodded and gave an order "Prepare for refueling and departure as soon as possible" and Ambassador Smirnov and his agents returned to the transit lounge to wait until their departure.

Annisa put her arm around Nina and led her to a seat in the gate area where Ruth and Helke joined them. The tension in the room began to dissipate. Vickie, George and Mark conferred with Colonel Suradji to make arrangements to hold Joe Forrest in the local jail until they could get him back to Jakarta. There would be many formalities in his future, and eventually a trial and imprisonment in the United States. As a traitor who sold his country's secrets in a time of war, he could expect no mercy.

Epilogue

Soft flickering oil lights illuminated the entrance to Annisa's house in Ubud, and the only sounds were the creaking and rustling of the tall bamboos surrounding the compound as they swayed in the night wind. Hearing Colonel Suradji's vehicles approach, the guard at the gate threw off his blanket and stood up from the threshold where he had been sleeping.

"Salamat tinggal! Welcome!" he said softly as the tired little group--Mark and Ruth, Helke, George and Vickie--arrived at the door, then stood aside to allow them to enter as the police vehicles departed. As they passed the spirit screen, they saw the large *balé*, brightly illuminated with candles, where a long buffet table stood loaded with food. Some of the house's community sat slumped on the steps, sleeping or chatting quietly as if waiting for the next act to begin.

"I am famished" said Helke "and I can't wait to sit down with a plate of food and go over the events of tonight! But first, I need to freshen up. I can still smell that van, and Khalid's sandalwood." She walked off in the direction of the small pavilion where she and Ruth had slept previously as two of the house's residents came to help. The others — Mark, George, Vickie and Ruth, waited to find out where they were to sleep.

Vickie, still wearing her tourist disguise, spoke up " George and I can share" she said, with a little proprietorial squeeze of George's hand and a sly glance at Ruth "we might as well get used to it." Ruth smiled at the implication of the double meaning: *"stay off my turf, Ruth!"* George looked a trifle rueful but said nothing. Together they walked off behind one of the women. "I can't wait to get out of this hideous outfit and into some decent clothes! See you all back here in fifteen minutes," Vickie said as they disappeared into the outer darkness.

Still sitting on the steps of the *balé*, Mark and Ruth waited to be told where they would sleep. Ruth said "Oh, Mark! What a wild time it's been! I'm glad you're here now!"

"Well, it seems to be over for now, and maybe we can get back to our own lives! Not that it hasn't been fun, Ruth, but I prefer a quieter life. And I want you back." Mark said.

Pausing for a moment and drawing a deep breath, Ruth spoke again "I've been doing some thinking, and we need to talk. It can wait till we're back home though to discuss it in detail, but here's what I want to do..."

Mark interrupted her "If this has anything to do with Stewart, there's nothing to discuss. I believe you that nothing happened between you. End of story."

"No -- not that. Nothing happened, nothing ever will." Then, smiling, "Vickie's going to see to that! I love you, Mark, and I want us to stay together but just being a foreign service 'spouse' isn't enough for me. I want to take the foreign service exam and try to upset the 'marriage rule'. Will you help me?"

He began to laugh: "Is that all? I thought you were going to ask for a divorce! But -- are you sure? I agree it's time the foreign service moved into the modern world, but you're up against a pretty hard-nosed bureaucracy, you know that!"

"Oh, I am very well aware of it, probably more than you are! But just think -- out with two-for-the-price-of-one! No more genuflecting to 'senior wives'! And we wouldn't be alone -- there's a wave of change coming, and together we could be part of it" Ruth's enthusiasm brimmed over "and, after all, we have two US ambassadors married to one another now! It's impossible to argue that a married woman can't do an officer's job with that example! So, what's the delay in extending it to the ranks?"

"As a matter of fact, I think that you and Helke just proved that married women can do an officer's job! So, I'll support you -- and we will just have to see how things go. First though, you gotta get through that exam, and I think you know how difficult it is!" he replied, as someone came to take them to their sleeping quarters.

Ruth, encouraged but a little disappointed, trailed him as she had done now for years, still holding the hope that equality would come eventually, and she would not always be the "trailing spouse."

A half hour later, cleaned up and refreshed, the group gathered again. Nyoman appeared in the *balé* as they began to help themselves from the buffet. "Annisa and Nina are on the way. The court has released Nina into Annisa's care. The immigration judge was a woman, very sympathetic to Nina's story, no worries at all there. She can leave Indonesia whenever she wants to."

"Have Ambassador Smirnov and his KGB thugs left yet?" asked Mark.

"Da", said Nyoman, with an exaggerated Russian accent "they didn't look happy either. Wonder what's waiting for them back in Moscow, without Nina?"

"Nothing good!" said George "You know, if that plane had arrived on time, Nina would be gone now." Turning to Ruth, he asked "Do you remember that little notebook that your cook found — the one with HC -- Nina's initials in Cyrillic -- written against yesterday's date?"

Reluctant to speak to George, but feeling obliged to, Ruth said "Yes. What of it?"

"We learned from Joe tonight that they planned to grab Nina that day, but they couldn't do it because they had no place to hide her until the plane arrived so they had to change their plans. Bit of luck for Nina and us!"

A little flurry at the doorway behind the spirit screen announced the arrival of Nina and Annisa. "Have you all heard? I can stay with Annisa, and leave Indonesia whenever I want to!" cried Nina, Still wearing the inappropriate red suit but with no other reminder of the stress of the past days, she moved swiftly to her friends. "The judge was lovely -- she agreed that I shouldn't go with Igor. So -- I am free! Free to be Nina!"

She sprang down from the platform to the floor of the courtyard, and, spinning, twirling, trailing bubbles of laughter behind her, she pirouetted around the courtyard.

Stopping in front of the group, she made *révérence,* the dancer's thanks to a teacher for the sharing of knowledge -- arms curved high, then lowered to the sides, she bowed her head, made a deep curtsey, straightened, and opened her arms wide in an inclusive gesture of thanks to her audience. More accustomed to expressing emotion through movement than speech, in a surpassingly graceful gesture she brought her hands together and pressed them to her heart, turning her head as she did so to look directly at each member of the group and acknowledge the bond of her obligation to them. Then, smiling, she resumed her formal position, holding it as if an imaginary curtain were descending.

Mark and Ruth, deeply moved, began to applaud in the slow rhythmic manner used by Russians to praise an extraordinary performance, and slowly the others joined them.

One by one the people in the compound slept, the night wind continued to rustle in the bamboos and stir the light hangings of the pavilions, an owl called from somewhere close by, and the peace of the Balinese night was unbroken. The Island of the Gods had regained its balance and successfully defeated once more the intrusions of the modern world, but for how much longer would it be able to hold them at bay?

9 781958 877777